For Agnes McCall, 'Aunt Agnes',
with much love

ALSO BY THERESA BRESLIN

A Homecoming for Kezzie
Death or Glory Boys
Whispers in the Graveyard

Kezzie

Theresa Breslin

EGMONT

Acknowledgement
The photograph used in the front-cover montage is reproduced with
permission of The Trustees of the Imperial War Museum, London

First published in Great Britain 1993
by Methuen Children's Books Ltd
This edition published 2002
by Egmont Books Limited
239 Kensington High Street
London W8 6SA

Text copyright © 1993 Theresa Breslin
Cover design copyright © 2002 Stuart Haygarth

The moral rights of the author and the cover illustrator have been asserted

ISBN 1 4052 0110 X

10 9 8 7 6 5 4 3 2

A CIP catalogue record for this title
is available from the British Library

Typeset by Avon DataSet Ltd, Bidford on Avon, Warwickshire B50 4JH
(www.avondataset.com)
Printed and bound in Great Britain
by Cox & Wyman Ltd, Reading, Berkshire

Contents

Preface

Juvenile Emigration was a phenomenon peculiar only to Britain, who sent overseas tens of thousands of children, some of them under the age of five, from Welfare Institutions.

It was truly believed that it would be in the best interests of the children concerned, and that they were being rescued from a life of poverty and squalor. This was often done without the knowledge or permission of any remaining family which the child might have.

Over one hundred thousand children were sent to Canada. This involved different schemes run by several agencies with varying degrees of care. The children could remain in orphanages or farm schools; they could be sent out as servants or placed for fostering. Some children did make a success of their new lives, settling in happily. Some did not.

Although child migration became increasing unpopular, it was not until 1982 that it became a legal requirement for voluntary associations to obtain the consent of the Secretary of State before sending a child abroad.

Part I

SCOTLAND

1. Canal trip

'Run, Kezzie, run!'

Kezzie could hear her little sister's shrill voice as she rounded the last curve on the field and saw ahead of her the rope, held at either end by the minister and the Sunday school teacher. Her bare feet thudded on the grass, dry after many sunny summer weeks.

Peg McKinnon, on her right, was still in front and running fast, her long plaits dancing at her back. Could she catch her? This would be her last year to run in the annual race. When the school started back after the holidays she would be a senior and much too dignified

for this. Her long brown hair flew out behind her. She
was aware her ribbon was loose, her yellow ribbon
which her father had tied in her hair that morning. Oh!
How she would love to win, and beat the long-legged
Peg just this once!

John Munro, a tall good-looking man of about
forty, stood with a group of fellow miners fifty yards
short of the finishing line. They were holding back the
rest of the younger children who would otherwise have
crowded on to the track.

'My money's on the tall one with the print frock,'
said the colliery foreman.

John Munro shook his head.

'The lassie with the yellow ribbon,' he said.

And, as his daughter drew level with him, he
shouted, 'Now, lass, now!'

Kezzie heard her father's voice beside her and she
thrust herself forwards. Head back, power surging in
her body, she flung herself at the finishing line.

'Yeeees!' Lucy was there, grabbing her legs, the end
of her skirt, anywhere, with her little fists. 'I knew you'd
win, Kissy. I just knew you'd win. I said so. I told

everybody. Didn't I, Daddy?' She held her hands outstretched as her father approached and he gathered her up and swung her across his back.

John Munro looked at his eldest daughter.

'We all knew,' he said quietly. He put his hands on Kezzie's shoulders. 'Hold still, now, while I fix your ribbon.' And he retied the bright yellow silk among the long brown curls.

They came home with all the rest down the canal in the coal scows, which had been scrubbed out by the carters and decorated for the occasion. The ponderous Clydesdale horses, beribboned and tasselled, made their way along the towpath. There would be a prize for the best decorated! Aunt Bella's husband always won. He spent long hours pleating and combing the horse's mane, intertwining lace, coloured wool and ribbon among the heavy glossy hair. One year he had even got Bella to knit the horse ear muffs! A huge purple plume nodded on its forehead. Bells and brasses, polished and shining, hesitated, then swung on, as they opened the bridge at Auchinmarloch. In the gathering dusk the scows glided through towards Stonevale and home.

'This has been the best ever,' said Lucy as she snuggled into her father's jacket. 'Hasn't it?'

John Munro glanced at Kezzie.

'What do you say?' he asked.

Kezzie smiled back. She loved the annual treat. The trip along the water away from the village and the grim grey houses of the next town of Shawcross, then out to the country. Tinnie round their necks, the children lined up for their lemonade, their bun, biscuit and rock cake. And then the competitions! Well, she had her prize, her pencil and book *and* her dad's team had won the tug-of-war, and Grandad . . . She glanced behind her. Old John Munro was having a great day too. Sitting in the back, a big slab of a man still, despite his white hair and moustache, red kerchief knotted at the neck of his collarless shirt, cap pushed to the back of his head, he was arguing, as always, with his friends.

'Nationalisation,' she heard him say. 'It's the only thing if mines are going to be modernised. The owners will never put money in for new machinery. We're years behind Europe. We're using the same wooden props that my father made; they've got conveyor belts and we're still using the ponies.'

'Well,' said another old miner sarcastically. 'If ye keep yer safety levels low it saves ye payin' off if there's a slump. We're in 1937 and there's thirty miners injured an hour. Nae compensation, a tied hoose and some still paid by piece rates. Ye canna win.'

'Amn't I the one who knows about no compensation?' said Kezzie's grandad indicating his crippled leg. Her grandad had been retired early from his job as a skilled engineer after an accident. 'That's why the pits should be nationalised,' he insisted, 'and, we will win. They tried to break our backs in 1926 in the General Strike.'

'Aye and did it too,' said one of the other men bitterly.

There was a silence.

'It's the Jarrow men I feel sorry for. There's nothing there for them.'

'Now there was a piece of chicanery, if ever there was,' said Kezzie's grandad. 'That's a classic case of owners looking after themselves. Palmer's Yard in Jarrow was bought out by a group of other shipbuilders and then to keep their monopoly they deliberately closed that yard down. An' I'll tell you what the President of the Board of Trade said to one group of marchers after the march to London, "Go back to Jarrow and work out your own salvation." And that's where they are yet. On the dole.'

Kezzie knew her grandad had been on one of the hunger marches to London and still got upset when he spoke about it. The marches hadn't seemed to affect the thinking of those in power, though she had been told that all the way down the long road south, people from villages and towns, some of them very poor themselves, had come out to give the men food and shelter. Already on Tyneside this decade was beginning to be known as the 'Hungry Thirties'.

'Trade's picking up slowly,' said another miner, 'if the appeasement policy wins through and there's no war with Germany and Italy we can progress internationally.'

'Appeasement,' snorted Kezzie's grandad. 'You don't appease bullies like Adolf Hitler and Mussolini.'

'Come on, Dad,' said Kezzie's father.

KEZZIE

:

The boat was tying up and already some of the windows were lit in the miners' rows.

Kezzie's father took Grandad by his sleeve. 'Time to go home now.'

2. Aunt Bella

'How do you spell "Kissy"?' Lucy asked on their way home from school one day a few weeks later.

' "*Kezzie*." How many times do I have to tell you?' laughed Kezzie. 'You're nearly six now, you should be able to say my name properly. K-E-Z-Z-I-E. Why do you want to know?'

'It's a surprise,' said Lucy. 'You've not to know about the cake.'

'What cake?'

Lucy put her hand to her mouth. 'You weren't to know,' she wailed.

'Know what?' asked Kezzie.

'Well, it's a secret,' said Lucy, 'but if you promise not to tell . . .'

'But it's me that's not to know,' Kezzie giggled. She regarded her little sister gravely. 'Can't you keep a secret?'

'I don't want to,' said Lucy, 'not from you. Grandad and I are making a cake for your birthday. It's going to have icing and your name on it. We're going to make it when you go to see the headmaster with Daddy, and then we'll hide it and it'll be a surprise for your birthday tomorrow.'

Kezzie shook her head and laughed as Lucy went skipping on ahead past the washhouses to play with her friends. Kezzie went on to their house at the end of the row. Her grandad was sitting at the door in the sun peeling potatoes.

'Aye, lass,' he acknowledged as she went indoors.

Kezzie had always thought of herself as lucky. Being at the end of the row their house had three rooms compared to the others with only two or even one. They had space to live with each other, some plain but serviceable furniture and pretty net curtains at the window. She put her books on the dresser and put on the cross-over flowery pinny, which had belonged to her mother. Then she set the big kettle of water to boil on the fire. She dragged the tin bath out from under the recess bed and put a towel and soap on the little stool, ready for her dad coming off his shift at two. She took his shifting clothes from the cupboard and hung them on the clothes horse to air. She caught sight of the photograph of her mother on the mantelpiece. She was said to resemble her mother, tall, with brown eyes and hair. She couldn't properly recall her, just remembered a special loving smell and someone singing when she was little.

Yes, they were luckier than most. Her father had never dropped a shift and with the money her grandad made doing odd jobs on a nearby farm they managed quite well. Well enough for her father to be able to let her stay on at school. Not so Peg, her great running rival, who had not returned after the summer holidays. Her parents did not think it was worthwhile for girls to be educated. Peggie was now working as a maid in one of the big houses along the main road and Kezzie saw her on her day off each month. She said she liked it fine and she got to keep a few pennies of her 'own money' and she acted so grown up, but Kezzie knew she had longed to stay on and go to college. Their teacher had called her a mathematical genius. She would have done bookkeeping and accounts. It didn't seem a lot to want.

Kezzie scraped the remains of the morning's porridge into a dish and put it on the dresser. With some warm milk it would do for supper for Lucy. She went out to collect the potatoes from her grandad. Aunt Bella was approaching, two children at her side and a cup in her hand.

'Uhuh,' Grandad grunted and got up. 'Here's Bella Borrow. She must have seen ye coming by.' He went to stand at the gable-end of the house to smoke his pipe.

'Eh, hello, hen,' said Aunt Bella glancing nervously towards the old man. 'I don't suppose you could spare a wee drop of . . .'

'Of course,' said Kezzie kindly. She knew that Aunt Bella's husband didn't earn as much as her dad and much of what he did never reached his wife, but instead found its way into the pockets of the innkeeper at the canal bridge. She went inside and took two sticks of liquorice from a little jar on the dresser and gave them to the children. Kezzie noticed the porridge.

'Would this be of any use to you?' she asked. 'I was going to put it out anyway.'

The older woman took the dish gratefully.

'You're a good girl, Kezzie, kindly, just like your mother was. She never turned anyone away. She would have been proud of you. The way you keep this house and look after the wee one. You're going to stay on at the school, I hear. That's a great thing for the likes of us. Aye, she would have been that proud.'

When Bella left Kezzie put the potatoes on to boil, and then sat down at the table and opened her school books. She chewed the end of her pencil and frowned in concentration. She was going to pass the exams. She wasn't going to let her father down and besides she had to get good grades if she was going to achieve her ambition. As yet she had told no one about it.

3. The silver locket

'Blow out your candles!' cried Lucy. 'And make a wish!'

Kezzie closed her eyes and wished.

'What did you wish for?' asked Lucy.

'You're not supposed to tell,' said Kezzie.

'But you can whisper it to me,' said Lucy. 'I won't let ANYONE know.'

Everyone around the kitchen table laughed as Kezzie cut her birthday cake.

'Did you see what Aunt Bella gave me,' Kezzie showed her father the leather-bound notebook. 'Isn't it beautiful?' She stroked the black binding.

Lucy opened it up.

'This book has no story,' she complained.

'I'll tell you a story before you go to sleep tonight,' said her father.

'Aunt Bella bought me the notebook for my school work. I'd better do some fine work in a book like this.'

Kezzie's grandad snorted.

'She'd be better off putting food in her bairns' mouths than running up her book at the Co-op on fancy presents.'

'Grandad,' said Kezzie gently. 'It's her way of saying thank you.'

'And here's mine,' said Kezzie's father interrupting. He handed her a little red box.

Kezzie opened it up. A dainty silver locket with a fine chain lay inside.

Kezzie had never seen, far less owned, anything like it. She felt her eyes fill with tears. She let the chain run through her fingers.

:

Her father took it from her and fastened it around her throat. He kissed the top of her head.

'You're a woman now. Happy fourteenth birthday.'

There was a soft knock on their door. Lucy jumped down from her chair and ran to open it.

A woman stood there with a baby across her shoulder, happed up in a plaid. By her side was a barefoot boy of about twelve. Their clothes were threadbare and they had a weary look.

'Your da at home?' the woman asked.

John Munro got to his feet at once.

'Come in, now, come in. There's some stew here, and milk for the baby.'

The travellers came regularly round the village but were not welcome at every door. The two of them sat down at the table, the boy on the very edge of the chair. The woman filled a bottle with milk from the jug on the table and began to feed her baby.

'Where's your man tonight?' John Munro asked.

'In jail, in Perth. Quadded for poaching.'

'Bad fortune,' said Kezzie's grandad as he ladled stew into two bowls.

'Shaness,' repeated the woman in cant, 'that allows one man to own the birds of the air and shoot them for sport, and another to be put in prison for trying to feed his family.'

She wrapped up her baby, lifted a spoon and began to eat her food slowly.

Lucy was staring at the boy.

'What's your name? Mine's Lucy, and this is Kezzie. She's my big sister and it's her birthday,' she said.

'Matt McPhee, miss,' the boy said, touching his forehead with his fingers.

'Would you like a piece of cake?' Kezzie offered him the plate.

His face flushed and he took the cake and carefully put it in his mouth.

The boy's mother took Lucy's hand.

'Let me see now, what good luck is coming your way.' She studied Lucy's palm carefully. 'A journey,' she intoned, 'a long journey, across the water.'

Lucy's eyes opened wide. 'Where?' she asked.

'That I can't rightly say, lamb. Only that it's a faraway country, and ye'll be going soon.'

Kezzie held her hand out. 'What about me?'

'Now, you're the same. A journey, in a great boat.'

'Oh, Kezzie,' cried Lucy. 'We're going in a boat together!'

'I didn't say ye'd be together,' said the woman slowly. She frowned and studied Kezzie's palm. 'You're with someone on this boat, but it looks like a young man.'

It was Kezzie's turn to blush.

'Is he handsome?' asked Lucy.

'Is he rich?' asked Kezzie's father.

'Aye, he's both,' said the woman. She took hold of Grandad's hand despite his protest. 'Now, here's an interesting hand, a long lifeline, and ye're going to meet a queen.'

Everyone laughed.

'Well, if the King and Queen ever visit Stonevale,' said Kezzie's grandad, 'I'll certainly be havin' a word with them.'

'I tell ye now. It's true,' the woman protested. 'There's a royal connection in your life.' She looked at her son. 'Am I ever wrong, Matt?'

The boy shook his head.

Kezzie's father stretched his hand across.

'Now, tell me I'm to meet a princess,' he laughed.

There was the briefest hesitation, then the woman slid her own hand under his and turned John Munro's palm face down on to the deal table.

'You have two beautiful princesses sitting right beside you at this very minute,' she said brightly. She exchanged a glance with her son.

He scraped his chair back quickly and stood up. 'Any work need doin', mister?'

'Yes, indeed,' said John Munro, pointing to a cupboard in the small hall at the front door. 'That press in the lobby needs filling with coal from the cellar, and my boots need a good dubbing. And there's a half-crown in it for you if I can see my face in the polish.'

Kezzie knew that her father was saving the boy's pride by giving him the work.

She cleared the table as Lucy got ready for bed. She could hear her dad and grandad talking outside with other miners as she washed the dishes at the window sink. As their house was at the end of the row it seemed the natural place for people to gather in the lighter nights. Kezzie knew it was also because her father and grandad's opinions were respected in the village. The men played quoits and smoked their pipes, soft curls of pungent blue smoke in the evening air.

'I don't know if I fancy these mechanical cutters,' one man said. 'I was talking to a man who worked with them down south and he said you're eating dust all the time, an' you have to shout to be heard. If you can't hear down a pit, you're in mortal peril.'

There was a murmur of agreement.

Kezzie remembered her grandad telling her about how clear his hearing became in the dark in the pit. How he could hear men who were working a seam a quarter of a mile away, talking and laughing. How he learned to listen for any movement, every small dark sigh of the earth, each little creak or groan, or dribble of shale; the miner's ear tuned for danger.

'Nothin' wrang wi' yer ain pick an' shovel,' said another voice.

'Aye, ye'll be carrying yer graith tae yer grave, Andra,' Kezzie's father joked.

Everybody laughed.

'The mines need to be owned by the miners,' said Kezzie's grandad. 'That's the only way we'll get decent conditions. Changing facilities at the pit head and the like.'

'We'll hae spray baths wi' hot water laid on for us, ye reckon,' said another.

The men all laughed again.

'Aye, ye can laugh. They'll be lookin' tae please us soon enough when they need the coal. Re-armament's started. There's a war coming.'

There was a silence.

'Well, war or no',' Kezzie heard her father say. 'I'm away in to put my bairn to bed.'

Kezzie made up her father's sandwiches for the next morning and packed them firmly into his rat-proof metal tin. She then made a treacle sandwich for Lucy's supper and set a little enamel mug of milk to warm at the fire. She combed the tugs out of her sister's blonde curls, and, winding some strands of hair round her fingers, she pinned a little cockscomb on the top of her head. Her father and Grandad came in. Her father sat down in the big chair and pulled Lucy on to his lap to read her a story. Grandad set out the chess board on the kitchen table.

'Are you for a game tonight, lass?' he asked.

Kezzie sat down. The chess pieces were very old, hand carved from wood and Grandad was the best player in five villages. He took his knight and bishop from the board.

'Right, now, let's see what you can do.'

4. Disaster

'Wait for me, Kissy, wait for me!'

Kezzie looked back down the hill where her sister and her friends were trailing a long way behind. She put the pail, half-full of bramble berries, on the grass and sat down to wait for them to catch up. Below her the little village trailed plumes of smoke, black and grey into the sky. The evenings were cooler, the sky a sharper, darker blue at night. Over to the left she could see the colliery, the wheel still, waiting for the shift changeover. In a few hours her father would be home, time enough to fill the pail for jam, if Lucy left any. Most times she had eaten half what they had gathered before they arrived home, her mouth stained with berry juice.

Kezzie lay down on the grass and squinted at the clouds. She liked to imagine places from their shapes. That one looked like India. She was going to go there one day. Her dream, her birthday wish. She was going to be a doctor, and then a missionary. After she had cured all the people in Scotland she would go to faraway lands. She had read about David Livingstone and Mary Slessor. She put her hand in front of her face and studied it carefully. She wondered what it was like to be a different colour. The only foreigner she had ever seen was the Indian who came round from time to time, selling goods from a large brown suitcase. He looked strange in his business suit with a heavy turban on his head. Stockings and ribbons and packets of pins, and little jars of cold cream to take wrinkles from your face. Bella always bought a jar of this, at the same time declaring, 'It's a bliddy big bucket of the stuff Ah need, with what Ah've to put up wi'.'

:

Kezzie looked again at the clouds. She put her hands behind her head and stretched herself out. She loved the berry time, hot days and soft warm evenings. It was very quiet. There was a terrible stillness between the earth and the sky. Then ... the world seemed to stagger, and she felt rather than heard a great muffled thump from beneath her. A dull thud which echoed inside her.

Kezzie sat up and instinctively looked towards the pit. Before her horrified eyes the huge whorl wheel started to creak slowly forward. She leapt to her feet knocking over the pail. Berries spilled out across the grass. She was halfway down the hill and running fast when she heard the siren sounding.

It was still wailing as she joined the group of villagers streaming towards the pit head. People had run out of their homes and washhouses, women with sleeves rolled up, men half-dressed. Old women with shawls flung about their shoulders, little children snatched from play and gathered up on the way. Kezzie jostled her way forward until she was at the head of the crowd and could see into the lamp cabin where the miners' lamps were kept in rows upon the shelves. She was hoping that her dad's lamp would be in its place. Perhaps he had taken sick and not gone down this morning? Maybe someone had asked him for a change, or there had been a flood or some other reason for a stoppage, and his shift wasn't in.

His lamp space on the shelf lay empty.

There was someone beside her in the crowd. It was her grandfather.

'His lamp's away,' said Kezzie, her chin unsteady.

Grandad put his arm around her shoulder and gripped her tightly. And they stood there with the rest and did what women and children and old folk had done for generations before. They waited.

And the waiting itself took its toll. Their wearied faces, in anxious lines, huddled into their shawls and coats. While the minister and the priest came and went among them, and the Salvation Army arrived with hot soup and kind words. Through the night and into a grey morning they waited with an occasional rumour scurrying through them like an agitated wasp.

At one point the crowd scattered as the rescue team

from Shawcross roared up with extra breathing equipment. Two ambulances arrived and stood by.

Kezzie was slumped, exhausted against Grandad, when they heard the three bells sound. The steel cable vibrated and then the cage began to rise.

There was a cry from someone at the front of the crowd.

'There's men coming up. They've got some out!'

The ambulances were loaded and pulled away quickly.

'A bad fall. A right bad fall. And then another,' Kezzie heard. 'No warning, just an almighty crack.'

'It's those props,' she heard another voice. 'Rotten timber props, should have been renewed years ago.'

There was confusion everywhere. Men being brought into sudden daylight, women crying tears of joy. Suddenly the crowd fell silent, then parted. Kezzie saw the section deputy coming towards them.

A voice in the crowd. 'That's a right bastard of a job he has to do.'

The official ushered Kezzie and her grandfather into the pit office.

:

'You've got bad news for me,' said Grandad.

'The worst,' said the deputy. 'Sit down.'

'I'll take this standing up,' Grandad replied.

'It's been restless all week, spitting and crackling,' said the deputy, 'but today, quiet . . . Aye, too quiet. We should hae kent. The whole length of the face took a seat. Caught Alec McKinnon and his son, and a lad from Shawcross. No hope for them. A lot of bad injuries with the rest trapped. John was at the heading with another group eating his piece. Him and Michael Duthie went back up. We said to wait, wait for the rescue equipment. He said they didn't have the time. He was right. Those others wouldn't be out alive if it wasn't for him. He had the last one in his arms, only a boy. He had just passed him back to me . . .' The deputy's voice cracked. 'The whole lot came down on him . . . He would know nothing about it, mind, if that's any consolation.'

He turned to Kezzie. 'Your father is a hero. There's men owe their lives to him,' he was saying. 'His section was clear yet he went back along the seam.'

Kezzie didn't understand. She gazed at him. If her father was a hero then where was he?

She turned to her grandfather.

'Where is he?' she asked desperately.

'Your dad is dead,' Grandad said stolidly. 'My son is dead.'

A vast void opened up in front of Kezzie. She tried hard to concentrate. She opened her mouth but no sound came out.

'Lucy?' She looked around her. Voices and faces were not matching properly.

'Bella's got her.' Her grandad took her arm gently. As if in answer to a prayer Bella appeared at the office door. She crossed quickly and gathered Kezzie into her arms.

'I'll take her away home with me.'

Kezzie's grandad nodded. He addressed the deputy.

'I'll go down and collect my son's body.'

The deputy wiped his mouth wearily with the back of his hand.

'I don't think you appreciate what it's like down there. There's flooding and a trace of fire damp.'

The old man smiled.

'I know exactly what it's like,' he said. He pointed to

his twisted leg. 'I got that in a fall the same as this one. Somebody pulled me out or I'd be there yet. My boy's not biding there.'

Old John Munro leaned over the desk and picked the deputy's own safety lamp.

'I'm going now to bring my son home.'

5. Eviction

They buried the four miners a week later in the cemetery at Shawcross two miles away.

Peg McKinnon's mother was too distraught to attend and the two girls, arms supporting each other, led the cortege through the town. Shopkeepers pulled the blinds and closed their doors as they passed. The streets were lined with silent crowds. Men took off their caps and women bowed their heads in respect. The weather itself appeared to take notice of the great grief that swelled through the whole countryside. A grey dreich sky hung over the mourners as they laid their loved ones to rest: John Munro beside his wife and the baby boy she had died bearing.

Kezzie was totally numb as she watched her grandad lower her father's coffin. The retiring hymn 'Abide With Me' still sounded in her ears, the soaring notes of the organ and the voices from the church, filled to overflowing, would remain with her a long time. Now she knew what her father had meant when he had talked about the price miners' families paid for coal. Far from getting it cheaper than others they paid for it in blood. Grandad had warned her against being bitter, and she knew her father would not have approved of the terrible rage she felt inside her. Her hatred of the whole world, which engulfed her from time to time. Bella had tried to help, despite being busy with her own children, watching her in sorrow unable to ease her grief. The older woman had seen all this many times before. She tidied the house and cared for Lucy.

And Lucy, poor little Lucy, who had not fully understood what had happened.

'But I do not want him to die,' she had said stubbornly on the night of the accident. She had looked at Kezzie uncomprehendingly. 'Doesn't God know that I do not want Dadda to die?'

And Kezzie saw then that she could not explain it away to the little girl. She would not accept trite phrases and meaningless words.

'Nor did I,' she had said finally, realising that indeed there were no words which would ease that pain, that great lonely grief. And the two of them had cried together and held each other close, against the dark and the fear and the cold that was both outside and inside their little house that night.

Peg came to her among the crowd as she left the graveside.

'I'll say goodbye just now, Kezzie,' she said. Her face was blotched and she had her hankie screwed up in her hands. 'We're moving to Glasgow to try to get work. My ma won't let my other brother go back down the pit, so we'll have to get out.'

'Will you write to me?'

'What address?' asked Peg.

Kezzie looked at her friend, not understanding. Peg knew where she lived. They were separated in the crowd before Kezzie could ask her what she meant.

It wasn't more than a few days before Kezzie found out the meaning of Peg's words.

It was early morning when a sharp knock sounded on their door. There was a smartly dressed older man standing there with a rough-looking man and woman and a group of dirty children.

She didn't have time to speak when the man with the suit said, 'Right now, girl, I want no trouble here. I'll give you twenty minutes, and these folk have to get in.'

'What?' said Kezzie.

The rough-looking man was carrying some heavy sacks. He pushed past Kezzie and dumped them in the hall.

'What are you doing?' asked Kezzie, her voice rising in alarm.

'Give them time now, give them time,' said the older man, but he kept his foot firmly in the door and the group of people tried to come into the house.

Kezzie stepped back and gripped the coat she had put on over her nightdress more tightly around her.

'What is going on?' she demanded.

'These are mine owners' houses, there's no one lives here employed by the mine now. You have to get out.'

'Get out? This is my home,' shouted Kezzie.

Bella came running out of her house at the commotion, curlers in her hair.

'You ought to be ashamed of yourself,' she said to the older man. 'The man o' this house is dead bare a fortnight and yer flingin' his weans on the street.' She set herself beside Kezzie and lifted her arm. 'Get away outa here.'

'Aye and that's two weeks' rent that's due,' the man replied angrily, 'and it's me that'll have to make it up. They got a letter sent. They should have been out already.'

Bella cast about for a weapon and spied the poker by the fire. She picked it up and advanced on the group.

'If ye don't move yourself from this door in ten seconds flat it's no a letter ye'll be gettin fae me,' she yelled.

The man hurriedly moved out and down the road a bit.

'You're only making it worse for yourself,' he said to Kezzie. 'I'll need to get the police.'

'If we have to go, then we shall,' said Kezzie with dignity. 'I must have missed your letter. I haven't yet opened all the cards and letters of condolence which came for us, and it may have been among them. I will pay you the rent due and we'll be out as fast as we can.'

She closed the door firmly and leaned her back against it. Then she caught sight of Bella, her face bright red, curlers falling out of her hair, with the poker in her hand and her nightie half open.

'Aunt Bella, you're not decent,' she gasped.

Her aunt looked down at herself and after a moment started hooting with laughter.

'Well,' said Kezzie wiping the tears from her eyes, 'I never thought I'd laugh again for as long as I lived. Did you see his face when you shook that poker under his nose?'

'I'd have laid it on him as well, and fine he knew it,' said Bella angrily. 'Ah kent him when he had nae backside in his breeks. Now he's a jumped-up factor tellin' decent folk what to do.'

The two of them worked quickly, laying out blankets and piling all the household goods in the middle, dragging clothes from the pulley, then gathering the corners and securing the bundle in a big knot. They waited until everything was done before waking Grandad and Lucy.

'See here, your Auntie Bella's got a surprise for you in her house,' said Bella rousing the child gently from her little box bed.

Lucy followed Bella next door at once while Kezzie went to wake Grandad.

He looked so old and thin, Kezzie thought, as she watched him hurriedly pull on his trousers and jacket. He seemed to have shrunk over the last days and looked to her to make decisions.

They managed to half-drag and carry their bundles to Bella's house. Her children ran to help them lift the table and chairs. Those and the dresser they put against the back wall of her house, with all their bedding piled on top. Grandad refused even a cup of tea.

'We'll not get lodgings with no wage coming in, and Bella has no room. I'll away to the farm and ask about and see if I can find something.'

Kezzie tried to put out of her mind what might

happen if they did not find something. There were hostels in Glasgow for destitute men. She had heard they were dreary places and people had to roam the streets by day. She would perhaps find somewhere as a maid with her keep as part pay. But what about Lucy? She would be farmed out to different ones who would take her for a short time and then . . . ? Kezzie set her chin. No one was going to put Lucy in a home, she was determined they would all stay together.

She went next door and collected their last few items. The fire, unattended, had gone out. It seemed appropriate. She took the clock and her mother's picture from the mantelpiece. Her father's pit boots lay on the hearth. She bent to pick them up.

'I'll gae ye somethin' for them,' said a voice from the door. It was the new tenant returned. 'I could do wi' a new pair.' He came in and surveyed them critically. 'Half a crown.'

Kezzie gasped at the effrontery. She snatched up the boots.

'They are not for sale,' she said angrily and marched out of the house.

6. The bothy

It was early afternoon before Grandad returned wearily to the village.

'The farmer's got a place he'll let us stay until we find something better,' he told Kezzie. 'I've tried everywhere else but things are bad all over. Everyone wants to help but they're all in the same boat.'

They put some essentials into bags and Bella promised to get their chairs and table brought to them.

'The farmer said it wasn't up to much,' warned

Grandad as they made their way on to the country road, 'just an old bothy, but I reckoned we ought to take it. If we don't, and the authorities see the bairn homeless . . .' he nodded at Lucy.

Kezzie realised Grandad had been thinking the same thoughts as she had. At this moment she didn't particularly care where they went. She wanted away from the rows before the early shift came home. It was more than her heart could bear to see the men trudging up the street and know her father was not among them. She pictured him so well, the muffler wound round his neck, cap pulled down, his face black with coal dust. For the last week or so Lucy and she had sat in the house at shift changeover, and as the tramp of feet went past the window the little girl would look up, and then slide silently over to stand beside Kezzie.

At the present time she was skipping along the road ahead of them picking flowers from the hedgerows and thinking this was a great adventure. Kezzie buttoned up her coat. The weather was getting colder. Well, at least they would be in shelter for the night.

'I think this must be it,' said Grandad eventually.

They stared across the field at a ramshackle little hut with a sagging roof. Kezzie felt her spirits sinking.

'Right then,' she said cheerfully. 'Over the gate,' and she lifted Lucy up.

They squelched through a rutted track to the bothy. There were holes in the roof, one wall was sloping gently, and the door, when she pushed it, gave way altogether and fell to the ground in front of them. Inside was an earthen floor with animal dung and broken pieces of machinery scattered around. The pane of glass in the one window had a long crack. Kezzie backed out of the doorway and laid her bags on the grass.

We can't stay here, she thought.

She turned to her grandfather. The old man was sitting on a large stone holding his head hung down in his hands.

It was Lucy who saved the day. She ran up to him with the bunch of wild flowers she had picked.

'Come on, Grandad,' she said, and threw her arms around his neck. 'You can pick a place for your bed. I've picked mine already. It's going to be under the window.

Come on,' and she tugged him to his feet and led him into the bothy.

Just as they crossed the threshold she repeated a phrase which she had obviously heard from the men talking outside their house in the past.

'See, Grandad,' she said firmly, 'you mustn't let the bastards grind you down.'

Kezzie's hand went over her mouth and she stepped smartly after her sister to give her a good smack for saying such a word. Inside the bothy Grandad was leaning against the wall helpless with laughter.

He wiped his eyes with the back of his hand. 'Did you hear that one?'

'I did indeed,' said Kezzie tartly, 'and she knows better than to use language like that.'

'Let her be,' he said, 'it's the smartest thing anyone's said all day. Look at her now. We'd best follow her example.'

Lucy was collecting all the pieces of junk and throwing them outside. It took them until dark. Grandad fetched his tool box and repaired the roof and fixed the door. Friends came down from the village with their other bits of furniture and stayed to help them. Kezzie told Bella to keep the dresser. By nightfall, a fire was going, the lamp was lit and the place was cosy. Grandad lit his pipe and looked about him.

'Well, it's not much, but it's home,' he said. He set the board out for a game of chess. Kezzie finished tucking Lucy up in bed.

'And we're together,' she added.

There was no question of her going back to school. Kezzie knew this quite well. The subject was never discussed. Who would she have talked to about it? Her grandad deferred to her in any decisions to be made. She was now the leader of her little family. He was up at dawn every day, tramping for miles, looking for any type of work. The farmer still gave him bits and pieces to do, but he had always earned small amounts, just enough for some tobacco and a bottle of beer. He came home with this little amount and put all of it in their money tin on the table. Occasionally there would be a ten-shilling note or a few pounds in it. It was some time before Kezzie realised what he was doing. Small objects disappeared, then their best linen sheets and one day, his good suit. She discovered he was walking to Glasgow and back to the pawnbrokers. One night he came in and sat down. He didn't look at her as he spoke.

'They're taking on for the tattie-howkin',' he said, eating his dinner and gazing stolidly at his plate.

Every autumn many children were excused school to help lift the potato crop. John Munro had never let his daughters go, he didn't want them to miss any days' study. Next morning Kezzie rose early and went to the farm.

The farmer scratched his head. 'Let me see,' he said, handing her a basket, 'where's the best place for ye?' He pondered a moment and repeated what she had said. 'You're fourteen years and this is yer first time liftin' tatties.' He shook his head in disbelief.

'I learn awful quick,' said Kezzie anxiously.

'Oh, aye, aye, aye. I ken fine who you are. John Munro's yer grandad. It's just that a lot o' the squads are made up lang syne . . . tell ye what, try yer hand wi' the Irish. A bundle o' them came off the boat fae Donegal last night, and they seemed short-handed to me.'

The Irish were singing in the field. And as Kezzie approached, her basket in her hand, she was aware of curious glances in her direction. The tractor was at the opposite end with a posse of gulls in attendance and Kezzie stood by the hedge not sure what to do, reluctant to interrupt. Their song rose to the sky in the clear autumn air, a lilting tune in Gaelic, which kept them in the rhythm of their work and a smile on their faces. And they worked hard. Kezzie saw this as she watched them move down the shaws, digging, lifting, swinging and emptying the heavy baskets.

'You're looking for someone?'

A woman had stopped beside her and addressed her in a soft accent.

'I've to work here,' said Kezzie. 'The farmer said . . .'

'Sure that's grand. Just you slide yourself in alongside Michael there,' the woman instructed her. 'And don't you be annoyin' that girl, now, Michael Donohoe,' the woman added as she noticed the wink the young man had given Kezzie as she took her place beside him.

She was utterly hopeless. Like a thoroughbred untrained for labour trying to pull a milk cart. The more she strained and tried to keep up, the worse she became. Clumsy, fumbling and inept, the other workers stepped politely out of her way and soon left her far behind. By lunchtime she was exhausted, and worse, she hadn't thought to bring any sandwiches. She had also dressed in completely the wrong clothes for such work. She sat down in the shade of a tree and thought what she might do. She would have to stay. Her pride told her that. That, and the empty money tin on the kitchen table.

'Is this space taken?' a voice asked. Kezzie looked up and the young Irishman, whom she had been placed alongside, was standing above her.

Kezzie shrugged and looked away. He was laughing at her. She was sure of it. His dark blue eyes in his brown face were full of devilment. She had often wondered why Aunt Bella stayed with her husband, or indeed had married him in the first place. Now and then, usually after 'a wee refreshment' Aunt Bella would tell Kezzie her life story. How, when walking out with various young men, her man had seen off all other competition. And it was due to his dark eyes, Aunt Bella would declare, full of mischief and life. Kezzie was sure that the eyes of Michael Donohoe showed that he was full of mischief.

'I wonder if you would do me a favour here?' he asked. He hesitated. 'You see, I've far too much food with me to eat today, and if I throw it away . . . well, beside being a waste, it encourages the birds, and then the tractor man will be in a dreadful rage with me.'

Kezzie turned and stared at him. He was all wide-eyed innocence. Did he suspect? she wondered. She would die of embarrassment if she thought that he had guessed that she had been so stupid as not to bring a lunch.

'You don't mind? Do you?' he enquired. And before she could answer he had put some sandwiches and an apple on the grass beside her. He saluted her and went away.

They resumed work after twenty minutes. 'I am

going to die,' Kezzie said to herself. She had never realised that potato picking was such hard work. She was absolutely determined to try to keep up but very soon thought, I'm going to fall over, and when I do, I will never get up again.

She was aware of someone humming quietly beside her. She glanced to her side, and through the rivers of sweat streaking down her hot face she spied Michael Donohoe.

'Good afternoon,' he said pleasantly.

She grunted in reply.

'Now we haven't been formally introduced,' he went on pleasantly, 'but I'm sure that you will not mind me mentioning this . . . After all I'm a stranger in a foreign land and you Scots are noted for your hospitable ways.' He paused.

Kezzie stopped and eased her aching back. If he was making fun of her, she would hit him over the head with the basket, she decided.

He placed his hand between her shoulder blades and rubbed gently.

'Begging your pardon,' he said courteously. He bent

down and placed her basket at a different angle. 'Like this,' he said, 'you stoop like this,' and he showed her how. 'Now I'll dig this row, and you follow after.' Then he moved on ahead of her using the graip, and she gathered in the potatoes behind him. She was aware that he was making slower time, but, as she could not move past him, she had no choice but to work at the slower pace he set.

They worked that way for the remainder of the day. He sang with the others, sometimes quietly as the work was hard, sometimes their voices rivalling the birds' evensong for harmony and beauty.

He carried her basket to the farm buildings for her, and then saluted and bade her good night.

Kezzie could scarcely walk the mile and a half home.

7. Potato harvest

Kezzie was at the field first the next morning and every morning after that, determined to show that she was as able as anyone else. And by some strange chance, no matter where she started off she always found herself working beside Michael Donohoe. And he always had a great story to tell her.

'Did I ever tell you about the time I was working at the fair in Ballyshannon, and the fellow with the dancing bear said to me, "Michael, hold this chain for one moment while I step inside this public house to wet my throat". And didn't the very next minute an old man with a barrel organ appear and start to wind the handle. And right away the bear put his arms around me, and there we were the two of us doing a jig down the main street.'

Michael stopped and wiped the back of his neck with his hankie.

Kezzie always pretended that his stories didn't interest her much.

'Mmmm?' she said, head down working hard.

'I never made as much money that day as I did any other. And the fellow comes out of the pub after an hour and gives me a shilling for minding his bear. But the sorrowful part of it was . . .'

'What?' Kezzie asked before she could stop herself.

'After that the bear wouldn't dance at all. Now at first we thought it was because it was all worn out with the dancing it had done that afternoon, because besides a jig, we had also had a waltz and a polka. It was a very educated bear, you see. But we very soon discovered it was a different reason altogether. And it wasn't until I ran into them a few weeks later at Limerick Fair and the poor man was pulling his hair out as he told me his story of how his bear would not dance a step . . . when suddenly the bear caught sight of me and leapt up and gave me a great hug. And then it was clear what had happened. The bear was pining away. And do you know the reason why?' Michael gave Kezzie a wicked look.

'No,' said Kezzie feigning indifference.

'Why that bear had fallen right in love with me.' Michael clasped his hands across his chest dramatically. 'Its heart was broken, don't you know?'

Kezzie grabbed a large potato and flung it at his head.

'I never heard such nonsense in all my life,' she said.

'You think it's nonsense that someone would fall in love with me?' he asked her slyly, his eyes bright and shining in his face.

'Perhaps not a poor dumb animal.' She pretended to ponder the question for a moment. 'No,' she said finally, 'even a poor dumb animal would have more sense than to fall for the likes of you.'

He began to walk her a bit of the road home at night and although she enjoyed his company she didn't want him to see the shack where they stayed. She always managed to put him off after a mile or so but he was a person who was not easily put off, and so she was not really surprised one evening just before sunset to see him coming across the field.

She sighed and went to meet him.

'I just happened to be passing,' he said innocently, 'and I thought I'd pay a call.'

'Come in,' said Kezzie, 'and meet Grandad and Lucy and I'll make you a cup of tea.'

Lucy took to him at once of course, and he told her three stories before she went to bed. About how he was a runaway son of the King of Ireland and lived in a castle with a drawbridge, and how he'd gone with gypsies and travelled all over Europe.

'Stop filling that child's head with rubbish,' said Kezzie eventually. She went with him to the gate.

'Where *do* you live, Michael?' she asked him. She imagined a whitewashed thatched cottage by the shores of a quiet beach. It was obvious to her the way the Irish workers spoke that they loved their country and thought it very beautiful. It must be disturbing to have to leave home every year for weeks in order to make some money to survive the winter. She had heard them use a saying which must be common at home. 'Donegal will never starve as long as there are potatoes in Scotland.' There was something wrong with the world, thought Kezzie, that most people seemed to have to break their backs for bread yet, day by day, in the newspapers and on the wireless all the talk of troubles in Europe meant that vast sums of money were being spent on building warships and making guns to prepare for a war against Hitler's Germany.

'Where do I live?' he repeated. 'I'm afraid that I don't live anywhere at the moment.'

She knew by his voice that this was not one of his stories.

'You and I are similar, Kezzie,' he said, 'in that we are orphans. I don't recall a mother or father. I just woke up one day in a children's home in Belfast. Except that no child should ever have been made to stay there and it certainly wasn't a home. And about four or five years ago, when I was about thirteen, it was Australia's turn for free child labour and I was one of the ones picked to go. I didn't know anything about Australia and I decided I didn't want to know either, so I ran away.'

'What do you mean "free child labour for Australia"?' asked Kezzie.

'There's not many people know or even care, but the British children's homes send children to their colonies. Now, lots of people leave their own country to go abroad where they hope they will live more easily. The Irish are famous for it. We are as the wild geese. But this is different. It is more of a compulsory emigration.'

'I suppose,' said Kezzie slowly, 'if you have no kin, and you're destitute it might be a better life.'

'But it's not only orphans that go,' said Michael, 'and they separate brothers and sisters, and they don't always enquire if there's family. These places have great power. They can take children from parents if they feel they are not being cared for properly, and then they think they own them.'

Kezzie shivered, thinking again about her own fears for Lucy on the day of their eviction.

'See, now in my case I did have some kin, only they hadn't bothered to tell me. It was just by chance that

I found out an old aunt of my mother's lived in Donegal. I stay there in the winter, though there's not much room.'

It was now quite dark. The stars were out and the harvest moon hung yellow and transparent in the sky.

'We have a sing-song in the barn the night before we sail,' said Michael. 'Will you come, with Lucy and your grandfather?'

'I'd love to,' said Kezzie. She hadn't realised the season had passed so quickly. She would have to think about work for the winter. They had saved a little but it wouldn't see them through. Besides Lucy had grown in the summer. Her coat and boots were far too small for her now.

She said good night to Michael. He hesitated for a second, then patted her on the head, vaulted over the gate and went off up the road whistling cheerfully.

8. Michael's farewell

They could hear the sound of music from the big barn as they came across the fields. Fiddle and accordion carried on the clear night air. Kezzie breathed in.

'Isn't it beautiful?' she said.

The moon was riding high in the sky and all the trees and bushes had an incandescent light upon them.

They had brought brown baps and scones, and little pancakes which Lucy had helped make. Her grandad had some beer, and everything was wrapped in a clean cloth in their basket.

Michael saw them and came over at once. He

looked very handsome with his white shirt and black waistcoat and his dark hair smoothed down.

'Come and sit with me,' he offered. He took Lucy by the hand. 'What have you in that basket, Careen,' he asked her. 'Anything for a starving man?'

'Pancakes, which I made myself.'

Michael clutched his stomach.

'Pancakes!' he exclaimed. 'How did you know that is my very favourite thing to eat.' He made smacking noises with his lips. 'Let me at them.'

'We have to put them on the table,' said Lucy primly. 'You will have to wait like everyone else.'

They laid their food out with all the rest on a trestle table which had been set up at the far end of the barn. There were plates heaped with potatoes, which had been baked in the open fire, bread and butter, cheese, hard boiled eggs, soda scones and a barrel of beer from the farmer.

'Now, isn't he the generous one,' Kezzie heard someone say.

And it was true. Some farmers did not like the Irish, saw them only as a source of cheap labour, to be used and got rid of as quickly as possible. Like the travellers, thought Kezzie. These two groups of people had similar ways, migrating across many miles seeking work. Most of the year they followed the harvests, from Ayrshire to the Lothians, down to the Borders and up past Perthshire. Even though many farms now used the new digging and haymaking machines, workers were needed for lifting the potato crop, and for turnip singling and mangel pulling. She wondered if she would enjoy it herself, this nomadic life, moving on at intervals, meeting different people. And what of those others, the emigrants of whom Michael had spoken? Those who left their homeland to become immigrants in a foreign country. What would it be like to be one of them? She supposed it would be interesting to learn about new and strange customs and have a chance of more prosperity. She would miss her own native land though, she knew that, the hills heather-purple and the village and its folk.

'Right, now,' said Michael. 'I'm going to teach you how to dance the "Walls of Limerick".' He grasped Kezzie firmly and swung her on to the floor.

And so the night passed. The Scots and the Irish with a common Celtic heritage in singing and dancing, sang and danced, mournful and happy by turn.

Lucy and Kezzie were flushed and exhausted after an eightsome reel.

'Wait now and I will get you a lemonade,' said Michael, and he went to fill up their enamel cups. Kezzie looked at where her grandad was arguing fiercely about something with a group of men. He hadn't enjoyed himself so much in weeks.

'Sing us a song, Michael,' someone called. 'Come on, now.'

Lucy leaned forward and tugged his sleeve.

'Make it a jolly one,' she said.

Michael winked at her. He stood in the middle of the floor, and bowed low. 'This is a song of special significance for a special person, not forgetting her sister.'

He hooked his thumbs into his braces;

> *Goodbye to all the boys at home, I'm sailing far*
> *across the foam*

To try and make me fortune in far Amerikay.
There's gold and money plenty for the poor and
  for the gentry
And when I come back again, I never more
  will stray . . .

Soon everyone was clapping and joining in.

So goodbye Muirsheen Durkin,
I'm sick and tired of workin'
No more I'll dig the praties,
No longer I'll be fooled.
As sure's me name is Carney,
I'll go off to Californay,
Where instead of digging praties
I'll be diggin' lumps of gold.

Lucy hugged him when he sat down.

'I liked that one, that was a nice song,' she said. 'Except your name's not Carney.'

'What did you mean, "it was of special significance"?' asked Kezzie.

:

'I'll tell you later,' said Michael. 'Come on.'

He pulled Kezzie to her feet and waltzed away with her to the 'Pride of Erin'.

'This babby is nearly sleeping,' said Michael softly as they reached the bothy.

It was after midnight and he had carried Lucy home with Kezzie walking beside him. From time to time they had stopped to look at the stars which seemed close enough to touch.

'I'm not a babby,' said a small voice.

'Deed you're not,' said Michael stoutly, and he set Lucy down gently. 'And if the big sister wasn't watching me, sure I'd be stealing a kiss from a pretty girl like you after walking her home on a beautiful moonlight night like this.'

He stole a sidelong glance at Kezzie.

'Be damned,' he said. 'I'm going to steal one anyway.' And he kissed Lucy on the top of her curly head. 'Now away to bed at once, before you drive a man wild.'

Lucy skipped inside laughing.

'I'll be there in a minute to tuck you up,' Kezzie called after her.

Michael turned to Kezzie.

'I'm not going home tomorrow with the rest,' he said.

Kezzie's eyes opened wide.

'Where are you going?'

'London.'

'But you hate the cities. You told me that!' she cried.

'Just for a few months. There's a cousin of my mother's there. He can fix me up. See, I'm planning to go to America and it's the only way I'll get enough money. Working the way I am now you only make enough to live on through the winter, and then it starts all over again. I've got to break the cycle and get out.'

'I know what you mean,' said Kezzie slowly. 'I've been thinking the same myself. We cannot live like this for ever. Lucy needs something better. I shall have to get some kind of steady work.

Michael fiddled with his shirt collar.

'You wouldn't think of America, yourself, would you?'

'America!' said Kezzie in amazement. 'America! What would we do in America? I don't know anyone in America.'

'Well, you might know me,' said Michael carefully.

'Oh.'

Kezzie looked into his dark blue eyes. He was not joking with her. His face was serious.

She didn't know what to say.

He put his hand on her shoulder.

'You might think on it,' said Michael. 'I'll come back and see you before I sail.' He grinned. 'Now, I'll have a kiss from the big sister,' and he brushed the side of her cheek with his lips.

Kezzie felt something catch at her heart.

She lay in bed with Lucy cuddled in beside her and gazed out at the moon through the little window. She heard her grandad coming home and going heavily to his bed. It was a long time before she fell asleep.

9. The rag doll

The weather became colder. The track to their home was now rutted mud and Kezzie felt the hard ground under her boots each day she walked out. Boots, which were now so small they cramped her feet badly and with soles so thin as to scarcely keep the damp out.

Each day she left Lucy at school and looked for work. Just before Christmas she was lucky and got some time at the pit head at the picking tables taking the rocks and the slats from the coal. She hated working there, hated the sound of the whistle, the noise of the bell and wheel turning, but it was all she could get. Grandad was having worse luck, Christmas was approaching and their summer savings and sacks of potatoes were running low. But with this job she could also bring home coal and it kept the hut cheery and warm.

'Do you think Santa Claus will know where we are?' Lucy asked anxiously one night.

'Santa knows where all good children are,' said Kezzie, not looking up from the sock she was darning.

Lucy climbed on her grandad's knee.

'Tell me a story,' she said.

Grandad reached for one of the books in the box beside the fire.

'No,' said Lucy, 'tell me the pony story.'

'Oh, that old story. You don't want to hear that again?' said Grandad.

This was just a routine they went through now and then, because Grandad knew that it was their favourite story. He let Lucy plead for a moment or two, and then, knocking the ash from his pipe against the chimney, he began.

'I was a pit lad at twelve. Did you know that?'

'Yes,' said Lucy snuggling in against his chest.

'Well, I was up at five in the morning and down the pit by half-past six, and it was a long long walk there and back, and hard hard work when you got there. But I looked forward to it every day of my youth, and do you know why? Because the best friend I had in all the world lived down that pit.'

Kezzie stopped her darning to listen.

'This friend's name was Meg and she was a beauty. She had brown hair and soft brown eyes, and as soon as she heard my voice in the morning calling her she would come to meet me. Now you might ask yourself what was a nice young lady doing living down a mine. Or perhaps you've guessed the secret already?' He bent his head and looked at Lucy.

'Meg was a pony!' Lucy cried.

'Yes, Meg was a pony,' agreed Grandad. 'And she wasn't just pretty, she had brains as well. And I'm going to tell you how I found that out.' He settled himself more comfortably in his chair.

'The ponies pulled the train of coal hutches backwards and forwards, the full ones from the face, the empty ones back, on separate lines. One day Meg and I were bringing the empties back along their rails when she stopped dead, and then crossed over on to the full track. Her ears were back and she was trembling. I was very surprised. Meg had never done anything like that before. And then I heard the sound of a runaway train!

I thought quickly. I couldn't tell which track they were on, but if it was the full one we would both be killed with the weight of the coal in the hutches. On the empty track we might get off lighter. I grabbed her harness and pulled her back over. The crashing noise of the wagons were almost on top of us when she tossed her head and, with me still hanging on her halter, landed us both on the full side. I screamed. I thought my end had come. Then the runaway wagons, five unloaded hutches, roared past us on the empty line.'

'And that,' said Lucy, finishing the story for him, 'is how a pit pony saved the life of a pit lad.'

After Lucy had fallen asleep Kezzie took out the rag doll she was making her for Christmas. She surveyed it critically. She had cut up a good cotton pillowcase for this doll and she was very proud of it. It was stuffed to a nice plumpness and had brown woollen hair, two blue button eyes and a stitched red smile on her face. Kezzie was now sewing her a dress and cape from an old tartan scarf.

'That's awful bonny,' said Grandad handing her a cup of tea.

She was knitting him a new muffler and had to snatch moments to work on it when he was out looking for odd jobs. He was even thinner. He hadn't managed more than a few shillings over the last weeks. It must be so frustrating, Kezzie thought, to have trained skills and only be able to mend bits of farm machinery from time to time. They were all less healthy than they had been. They couldn't afford to keep the fire burning all night, and Lucy had developed a wheeze and cough.

Kezzie worried about her extravagances, but when Christmas came she couldn't resist using most of their savings to make it special. They had a small chicken and cake to eat. She had filled their stockings with little things, tangerines, sweeties, some ribbons. She bought Grandad a bottle of beer and some tobacco, and Lucy gloves and a bonnet. Lucy had made them both hankies in school with their initials embroidered on. Grandad, too, had squandered his money and proudly brought out two books, a flower fairy story for Lucy, and *Catriona* for Kezzie. Grandad put his muffler on at once and insisted on wearing it while eating his dinner. Kezzie watched anxiously as Lucy pulled the doll out of her stocking.

'Look what Santa gave me!' she cried. She kissed it again and again. 'This is the most beautiful doll in all the world,' she said.

'Have you given her a name yet?' asked Grandad at night when she was in bed with her doll tucked up snugly beside her.

'Her name's Kissy,' said Lucy.

Later Kezzie was glad she had spent the money. In the grim days ahead she would look back often and remember that Christmas day and the warm glow it gave her helped her struggle on.

10. The pit boots

Coming back from the outside privy in the half-dark one morning Kezzie saw a large brown rat sitting on their table cleaning its whiskers. She shrieked and it ran away, scuttling across the floor towards the fireplace. She shivered and got back into bed beside Lucy. She could not fall asleep again. Hunger was gnawing at her. She had rationed out supper in a very miserly way last night and her small piece of bread hadn't filled her stomach at all. The child beside her whimpered softly in her sleep. She had been doing that a lot recently.

:

Kezzie lay and tried to think of the most economical way of using the few shillings they had left. She and Grandad had found no work at all that week. After Christmas no one had anything to spare and the little errands she had run for coppers were now not needed. They cut logs from the nearby wood to save coal, but it took up so much time and the wood burned quickly and gave off little heat. Grandad had taken the clock from the mantelpiece the week before and now she knew there was only one other thing they might get money for.

In the early afternoon she knocked on the door of the house that had once been hers. It was a sorry sight that she saw when the woman opened the door to her. The floor was littered and the range that she had black-leaded so lovingly was tarnished and dirty. The man pushed his wife out of the way.

'Oh, it's you,' he said. 'Ye've come back. I thought ye might.'

Kezzie held out her father's pit boots.

'I'll give ye a shilling for them,' he said.

Kezzie was dumbstruck. A shilling! She had

thought that he would offer less when she went back. But a shilling!

'D'ye want me tae make it sixpence?' he enquired roughly.

She put the boots down on the ground, took his shilling and turned away, walking blindly down the road.

'Lassie,' she heard someone call before she had gone very far, 'lassie.'

She turned and the woman of the house was coming towards her. She looked around her furtively and, taking a paper bag from under her shawl, she gave it to Kezzie, then hurried away. In the parcel was the heel end of a loaf and a piece of cheese.

The next day Kezzie went to see Bella. She knew her husband had been laid up for some time and he had no pay, but Bella was a picker at the pit head and at least she had something. It was in Kezzie's mind to ask her to take Lucy in for a time.

'Amn't I glad to see you,' declared Bella putting the kettle on at once. 'That one next door is always in here borrowing and her hoose! Well . . .' She stopped, sensing that Kezzie was upset. 'What's the matter, pet? Are things not so good with you?'

'Not very good,' said Kezzie. In the past she had never let the older woman guess quite how bad things were with them.

'You can sell stuff at the pawn, ye know. Ye mustn't be too proud. That good suit of ma man's has been up an' down that road so often, it kens the way to go itself.'

Kezzie laughed.

'Aunt Bella, we've pawned everything we can. I sold my father's pit boots to him next door yesterday.'

'My God, lassie, I didn't know it was as bad as that with you.' She twirled her cup in her hands for a minute or two, and then said, 'Have ye been tae the minister?'

Kezzie looked at her.

'Go on the Parish Relief? I couldn't.'

The older woman studied the floor for a moment. Then she sighed.

'I have,' she said.

The minister was setting his dinner on the table when

:

Kezzie knocked at the back door. Two small potatoes, a drop of stew and a bit of bread were on his plate. He's not doing much better than us, Kezzie thought, as he made her welcome and sat her down.

'I can give you a three-shilling allowance each time,' he said. 'I know it's not very much, but I have to keep to the rate. I must be fair. There are so many, and I must make sure every person gets something.' He looked at her kindly. 'I had no idea things were so bad with you. You should have come sooner.'

He insisted that she ate the food on the table, saying he had more in the pot. She didn't really believe him, but she was so tired and hungry that she did as she was told. She hadn't tasted meat for some time and she chewed it slowly. He brought through a ledger and entered the family details.

He closed his book and said gently, 'You know . . . your grandfather would get a place in a hostel in Glasgow, and some of the children's homes can be quite nice. I'm sure Lucy would adapt very quickly . . . and then I could probably find you a place as a stay-in scullery maid in one of the big houses. You would win

:

through, I'm sure. I remember your mother and father. You Munros have all got such a strong spirit.'

'No,' said Kezzie firmly. 'No.'

His mentioning her father gave her strength. 'Lucy wouldn't adapt. She would break her heart, and it would crush Grandad completely, and me . . . why, I would lie down and die. The reason we have such a great spirit is because we're together. We are a family.'

The minister nodded his head and smiled.

'I thought that would be your answer. You're a brave girl. Have you been to the mission in Shawcross?' he asked her.

She shook her head.

'They give out necessities, like tea and margarine. I'll write you a letter.'

She read it as she walked home.

'This is to certify that the bearer of this letter, one Keziah Munro of this parish, is destitute. She has two others in need of support and requires any such goods as you may give her.'

Kezzie folded the letter very carefully and put it in her pocket.

:

It was true then. It was written down. She was destitute.

11. Starvation

Kezzie left Lucy at school the next morning and walked to the mission at Shawcross. There was a queue of people waiting to be served at a counter at the far end of the hall. There were some very rough and dirty people jostling along in the group, folk with threadbare and greasy clothes. She tried to keep her distance as they pressed up against her. She waited in line for nearly an hour. When it came to her turn a very severe-looking woman behind the table put out her hand.

'Book,' she snapped.

:

'Book?' Kezzie repeated. She hadn't noticed that the others had a book which they handed over. 'I don't have a book.'

'No book. No goods.' The woman looked beyond Kezzie. 'Next.'

'I have a letter,' protested Kezzie. 'My minister said if he wrote a letter . . .'

'You need a book,' said the woman, already dealing with the next person. 'We need to mark in the date and what goods you receive. You only get a certain amount each month. Otherwise people like you would be in here every day getting stuff for nothing.'

'I'm sorry,' said Kezzie politely. 'Where do I get a book?'

The woman ignored her while she served three other people and then said, 'Go to the office.'

'Where is the office?'

Again she made Kezzie wait for a few minutes, then said, 'In the corridor. You must have noticed it on your way in.'

Kezzie returned to the corridor and found the office. It was closed. The notice on the door read OPEN

:

MONDAYS AND WEDNESDAYS. Today was Thursday. In order to get a book for rations she would have to wait four more days. Kezzie went back into the hall. The queue was now double the length. Kezzie marched to the front.

'Excuse me,' she said, placing herself directly in front of the woman. 'The office is closed.'

'Is it?' was the reply. 'Then you'll have to wait until it opens.' She snapped her fingers for the next person to come forward.

Kezzie side-stepped smartly and blocked them off.

'I can't wait four days,' she said. 'The reason I have the letter is because I am desperate.'

'You should have thought of that sooner, miss,' said the woman, 'before you let yourself get into such a state.'

Kezzie gasped.

'Do you think I want to be like this?' she said. 'To come here and have to beg from someone like you.'

'You be careful, madam. Talk that way to me and you'll get nothing. Now stand aside and let me deal with these people.'

The people who were waiting had become very quiet as they listened to this exchange of words.

'I will not stand aside. I was told to come here for food and I'm not leaving until I get some.'

The crowd murmured its approval.

The woman hesitated for a second. 'If you are really so desperate you can wait until the end. If there is anything left you might get something.'

Kezzie swallowed and tried to keep her temper. She thought of Lucy, with her outgrown boots and coat, and her thin peaked face. She thought of her grandad, away from early morning until nightfall each day and coming home with pennies. Her hand closed around the minister's letter.

'Damn you!' she shouted. 'Damn you to hell's fire! Keep your food. Keep your stupid book. I'll do without it!' And she crushed up the letter in her fist and threw it into the woman's face.

She ran outside. She could still hear the cheering and clapping from inside the hall, as she stamped down the street, an angry fire inside her. She knew that she had done something really stupid and would regret it later, but at the moment she didn't care. No human being should have to crawl to another, especially not for food.

'Miss, excuse me.'

Kezzie stopped. Someone was calling after her. It was an older woman, carrying a baby.

'Miss,' the woman hesitated, and, as she came nearer, Kezzie saw that in fact the girl could have been scarcely twenty.

'Miss, I heard what happened inside there. The Salvation Army give out soup and bread every day at their place, and they have clothes . . . if you need them.' She touched Kezzie on the arm lightly, and was gone.

This incident, instead of cheering Kezzie, made her feel even lower. The thought of queuing at a soup kitchen was too much to contemplate. People should be allowed to keep their dignity and not be humiliated, she thought, as she turned the corner into the main street. With this in her head it was just the wrong moment for her to catch sight of her grandfather.

At first she didn't realise it was him. What she saw

ahead of her in the street was an old man standing with his head down and his cap outstretched in his hand. A woman dropped a copper in, others walked past ignoring him, then one man pushed him roughly aside. Kezzie retreated a few steps and then turned and fled. She got round the corner and hurried away as quickly as she could through lanes and back alleys praying that he had not seen her.

The next day was bitterly cold, and Lucy protested strongly as Kezzie tried to force her feet into her little boots. They were far too small for her. Kezzie had at last to admit to this. She found a pair of her own from last year that she had outgrown and by putting a pair of Grandad's socks on Lucy's feet and stuffing the toes with paper she fitted them on her sister. They set off for school. Kezzie was in an ill humour. The events of the previous days and her sister's complaints had brought her down completely. The very sight of the child wrapped up with a huge wool scarf against the cold, with her skinny arms sticking out of her outgrown coat sleeves, stumbling along in the big boots, enraged her. Lucy was walking far too slowly and would be late for school. Kezzie wrenched cruelly at her arm.

'Hurry up,' she snapped.

Lucy pulled her arm away. 'I can walk to school myself,' she shouted, and with as much dignity as she could muster clumped determinedly off up the road.

Kezzie walked six miles into another town that day. She couldn't risk seeing her grandfather begging in Shawcross. She got nothing at all until almost closing time when a greengrocer said to wait behind and help shut up the shop. She dragged sacks of potatoes and boxes of apples and vegetables in from the street, then swept the floor. The man was kindly enough and gave her a bag of bruised fruit and vegetables as well as her money to take home. As she left the shop she saw her reflection in the lowered blinds. She looked unkempt, her hair was matted, her coat stained and missing a button.

It was a long six miles home in the dark carrying some boxes the shopkeeper had given her for firewood. When she arrived at the bothy the fire was barely burning and Grandad and Lucy were sitting at the table waiting for her.

'Have you not eaten?' she asked sharply.

'We were waiting for you,' said her grandfather. 'You are late, we were worried something was amiss.'

Kezzie crossed to the fire and threw another log on.

'And would you just sit there all night,' she cried, 'and let the fire go out and never think to make yourselves something to eat?'

Lucy opened her mouth.

'You be quiet,' said Kezzie. 'I've had enough of your moaning for one day. No one does much here except me, and I'm sick and fed up with it all. Look at this place. The roof is leaking and the wind is blowing in through the walls.' She glared at her grandfather. 'It's time you did some repairs around here instead of traipsing all over the town each day for no good whatsoever.'

He lowered his gaze and looked away. Kezzie began to set out cups and plates noisily on the table. She caught sight of her hands, chapped and red, her fingernails dirty and broken. She realised with a sudden shock that she was just like the people she had waited with in the queue the other day. The people she had moved away from and tried to keep at a distance. She roughly pulled open the drawer of the kitchen table to take out the breadboard and knife. The handle came away and dropped painfully on to her foot.

'This is exactly what is wrong!' she shrieked. 'Someone should have fixed this handle. It has been loose for weeks and neither of you would think of doing something about it.' She drew in a deep breath. 'You,' she pointed at her grandfather, 'get your toolbox and fix this and anything else that needs fixing. You,' she addressed Lucy who had gone to stand beside her grandad, 'get that grate cleaned out and this table top scrubbed and then bring out your sum book. You haven't done any school work for weeks and it's time you started.' She pulled a piece of bread for herself from the loaf and snatching up her coat she opened the door. 'I'm going for a walk and this must all be done when I come back. That is if I decide to come back at all.'

Kezzie walked in the woods for nearly two hours. It

:

was a clear and beautiful winter's night, with frost sparkling on trees and grass, but she did not see it at all. Her thoughts were confused and desperate. She knew that they were at the end of their road. Her outburst tonight had shown that. They had had arguments and fall-outs before like any normal family, but tonight had been different. She waited until Lucy and Grandad would have gone to bed and then returned home.

They were waiting for her when she softly opened the door. The fire was burning brightly, the grate swept and the table clean. Grandad was leaning over Lucy and her school books. They regarded her silently as she stood at the door.

'I'm sorry,' said Kezzie, and burst into tears.

She didn't know quite how it happened but next she was settled on Grandad's knee in the big chair by the fire with his arms around her, and Lucy brought her her doll to cuddle.

'Here,' said her sister generously, 'you can keep Kissy tonight if you want.'

Later with the doll cuddled between the two of

them Kezzie prayed: 'Dear God help us. If you don't do it soon then we surely will starve.'

And starve they would have if it had not been for the timely arrival of Matt McPhee.

12. Matt McPhee

A few days later Kezzie awoke suddenly in the early morning. She reached blindly for the small stone she kept on the floor beside her bed in case she ever saw a rat again. Nothing moved inside the bothy.

She got up quietly. Something or someone was creeping around outside, she was sure of it. She cautiously opened the door. In the half-light she saw, lying at her feet, a dead rabbit.

'Something wrong?'

Her grandad was beside her.

'Look.' She pointed at the ground.

:

Grandad stepped outside and glanced about him. There was no one in sight. Then a low whistle sounded from beyond the trees. Kezzie's grandfather raised his arm in a salute, and picking up the rabbit, he came back inside.

'It's the travellers,' he said.

They had rabbit stew at seven o'clock that morning, and all of them ate fit to burst.

'My tummy's sore,' said Lucy happily.

'Don't you DARE be sick,' said Kezzie laughing. She stirred the pot on the fire. 'There's enough here for tonight, as well.'

'I'll get some potatoes from the farmer today,' said Grandad, 'and we'll manage rabbit soup with them tomorrow.'

Kezzie had persuaded her grandfather to go back to the farm and ask for employment. He repaired the tools and machinery. Kezzie was sure that the farmer was only making work for her grandad out of friendship and pity, but she didn't care. It was better than letting Grandad go back to the town to beg. Even if he couldn't pay, the farmer always gave them milk

:

each day, and some potatoes or turnips to get by on.

Kezzie had also set Lucy little tasks to do in order to keep her occupied. No matter how tired or hungry she was, Lucy had to keep a jam jar on the table filled with fresh evergreens and berries. Her school work, which had been neglected, was now done every night, and Grandad was teaching her to play chess.

On the third day, when they had finished the soup, Kezzie opened the door in the morning to find a small chicken there. And so it went on. Every few days something was left, two plump pigeons, fish, eggs, then a fine buck hare which lasted them nearly a week.

The wind shifted round and there was a tingling in the air, as Kezzie got Lucy dressed for school one morning. She had gone previously to the Salvation Army clothing store and managed to find a pair of boots to fit her sister. She wrapped her up well and they were about to go outside when the door opened and in stepped Matt McPhee.

He touched his forehead, but did not speak.

Kezzie realised that it was a sign of respect. He was waiting for her to greet him first.

'Come in, please,' she said. 'Would you take some tea?'

He nodded and sat at the table.

'Matt,' said Kezzie as she poured his tea and cut him some bread. 'We want to thank you for your gifts.'

His face reddened and he concentrated on his cup.

'No, truly,' said Kezzie. 'These last days, you have stood between us and starvation.'

'As you did with us in the past.'

'How did you know that we needed help?' asked Kezzie.

'We had finished the berries at Blairgowrie and were on our way north. We met up with cousins at a camp in Brechin and they said they had been past this way. They had called at your house and had abuse and a shoe thrown at them. We knew that your da would never do that. He was a gentleman, your da. It's not a big house or money that makes you gentry. My mother sent me back down the road to see what was amiss.'

Kezzie suddenly remembered the travellers' last visit and Matt's mother telling their fortune.

'She knew, didn't she? Your mother knew?'

:

Matt looked away and then back towards them. He shook his head.

'Not exactly, no, or she would have warned you. She just told me that your da's hand was cold, very cold.'

There was a silence. Matt finished his tea and wiped his mouth.

'I came to speak with you as I'll need to be going back up the road soon. We always winter in Skye and I've got to get my two hundred days' schooling or the Cruelty fine us.'

Kezzie felt as though she had been struck.

'Go away?' she said.

'Aye, but before I do we will have to sort you out a bit better.' He stood up and glanced around him critically. 'This is a hole you're in and the snow's coming. I can smell it in the wind. I've sent word to other kin of ours in the Borders and we should get you fixed up with something else soon. Also, after you leave the bairn off to school I'm going to give you some real education. The kind that you don't learn from books, but it'll keep you 'til springtime.'

And that is what he did. Over the following days he

showed Kezzie how to live as well as nature would allow, how to rob a nest and set a snare, which berries were edible and which were not and how to follow animal tracks.

One afternoon just after Lucy had returned from school he appeared with a great smile on his face.

'Come quickly,' he said, 'and see what I have got for you.'

He led them to the other side of the wood, near where a clear stream ran.

'This is a better place for a camp,' he said, 'less damp, fresh water, and look . . .'

Parked beside the burn was an old-fashioned gypsy caravan.

'The man who had this has a modern trailer now, pulled by a car, would you believe?' Matt laughed. 'Not for the likes of me I'll tell you. I'll have a yoke and a tent any day. Anyroad, it's yours and it has a stove and a sink and all, it's watertight and it's up off the ground.'

'It's wonderful,' said Kezzie. The thought of leaving the bothy overjoyed her. She would get their things together at once and settle there tonight.

:

Matt seemed restless and she turned to speak to him.

'The people who brought this are waiting for me at the end of the lane,' he said. He held his hand out awkwardly. 'I must say goodbye.'

Impulsively Kezzie went forward and hugged him, not caring that he was rigid with embarrassment.

'Thank you, Matt McPhee,' she said, 'and tell your mother thanks. And may we have better fortune when we see you again,' she called after him as he ran off down the road.

13. Kezzie plays a trick

They settled themselves in the caravan and, as Matt had predicted, the snow came. They awoke one morning to that particular brightness and strange quietness that tells of a heavy fall of snow during the night. Lucy was delighted.

'No school!' she squealed and pulling her coat on over her night clothes she ran out to play.

And eventually, with not much persuading, Grandad and Kezzie joined her. For a few days while the first fall lay white and clean, Grandad and Kezzie gave up their search for work. When Kezzie thought about it later, she felt that their temporary return to childhood had been good medicine for both of them. They made snowmen and had snow fights, tried skating on a nearby frozen pond and even attempted to build an igloo.

At last a thaw came and with it the very first frail snowdrops scattered under trees and hedgerows. Kezzie felt better. The indication that the year was on the turn gave her hope, and as if to prove her right, Bella arrived breathless one day with what she hoped was good news.

'The new knitwear factory in Shawcross,' she gasped, out of breath with hurrying, 'they're hiring tomorrow at ten o'clock.'

Kezzie rose early and set out for the town, aiming to be there by eight o'clock, in plenty of time as she thought. She was aware of the noise as she approached the site but was totally unprepared for the crowds of people already gathered and waiting. She cursed her own foolishness for not thinking ahead. Some, obviously really desperate, must have been waiting since before dawn. Was she not really desperate? She asked herself this in anger. She estimated the crowd to be around three or four hundred. They were taking on, how many? Fifty? One hundred? No more certainly. She leaned against the wall and tried to think, hardly aware that she was fingering her silver locket. Your brain is in charge of your body, not the other way about, her father used to say. Use your brain.

She detached herself from the wall and hurried back the road she had come. She reached the Manse just as the minister was entering. He had been sitting all night with a dying old man whose family had all gone out to Australia. He heaved a sigh as he hung his coat and scarf on the hallstand. 'One of the sad things about emigration,' he said, 'is that it can break family bonds. When the young ones go off there's no one left at home to care for the old.'

'I'll not keep you one minute,' said Kezzie, and explained why she had come.

He wrote the letter of reference as she asked and handed it to her. She hesitated.

'Would you put it in an envelope please? And,' she added as he did so, 'will you address it "BY HAND, THE MANAGER"?'

He smiled.

'I can do even better,' he said, and sealed it with red wax.

Kezzie next went to Bella's house.

'Have you anything I can borrow?' she enquired. 'Something to wear to make me appear older?'

A wistful look came over her aunt's face.

'I may have the very thing,' she said.

She pulled an old kist from under the recess bed and took out a dark blue two-piece suit. It had a fitted jacket with a peplum waist and a long accordion-pleated skirt.

'This was the costume I was married in,' said Bella.

'I can't take that,' Kezzie protested.

'Why not?' asked Bella. She indicated her ample figure. 'It's never going to fit me again.'

She found a pair of black shoes with heels and little bows at the front. They were slightly large but stuffing the toes made them stay on Kezzie's smaller feet.

'Mmmm,' said Bella, walking round Kezzie and examining her carefully, 'a bag and, I think, some make-up.'

They found a purse-style handbag and Bella combed Kezzie's chestnut hair and pinned it up into a French roll. She then carefully applied make-up and some lipstick and rouge.

'Right,' she instructed, 'you go in there and kill them dead.' She threw a shawl about her shoulders and postured about the kitchen giving a display of how she imagined famous film stars acted. She puckered her lips together and minced up and down. 'Now, just you bat yer eyelids, pet, and if it's a man give him one of yer big smiles. Oh, and don't forget, wiggle yer bum a wee bit as ye walk across the room. Men like that.'

Kezzie ran all the way back to Shawcross. She knew that she had to get there before the factory opened at ten. It was just a few minutes to the hour when she reached the site again. She took a couple of deep breaths and walked purposefully to the head of the queue.

'Excuse me,' she said to the people at the front, 'I have a letter to deliver.'

She rapped on the door set in the wooden gate. No

one came. She tried again for longer and louder. After a pause a shutter slid back and a face appeared.

'We're not opening until ten,' a man said roughly.

'I know,' said Kezzie pleasantly. 'It's just that I was sent with this letter.'

'Give it to me then.'

'I was told to deliver it personally,' said Kezzie firmly, pointing to the writing on the envelope. 'There's something I have to explain.' She gave the man her brightest smile and tried to appear calm.

He hesitated, then opened the door a crack. She was in!

Kezzie hurried to the office buildings. Out in the yard she heard them getting ready to open the gate. There was a door marked SECRETARY. For a second she faltered, then went past it to the one marked MANAGER. She knocked briskly and walked straight in.

There was a small bald-headed man sitting behind a desk. He was dictating to a lady who was writing in a note pad. They both looked up in surprise.

'Oh! I do beg your pardon!' said Kezzie as politely

as possible. 'I thought this would be the office for the interviews. Did I make a mistake?'

The man consulted his pocket watch.

'Goodness it's ten o'clock already. I didn't realise.' He stood up. 'We'll continue later, Miss Dunlop. I'd better see these people right away.' He glanced out of the window to where the queue was assembling in the yard. 'Some of them have been waiting since before dawn.'

He indicated for Kezzie to sit down.

'Now what experience have you had with knitwear machines?' he asked her.

Something about his manner gave Kezzie a clue to how to react. She looked him straight in the eye.

'Absolutely none,' she stated truthfully. 'However, I do learn extremely quickly. I was intending to go to university but my father's death prevented that. I have my leaving certificate and a very good reference from my minister.' She handed him the letter.

He examined the seal carefully before opening and reading it.

'Very impressive,' he said. 'It says here that you are

diligent, truthful, hardworking, intelligent, punctual and of a neat and tidy appearance.' He smiled. 'Do you agree with all of this?'

'Yes,' said Kezzie.

The manager laughed out loud.

'How could I not employ you?' he asked. He took a card and wrote her details down. 'You start on Monday. The shift is eight o'clock until five thirty, with an hour for lunch. Tea is for sale but not food, so bring sandwiches.'

Kezzie stood up.

'Thank you very much,' she said.

'Don't you want to know what the wage is?' the manager asked her.

She blushed and sat down again quickly.

'You will start on the coarse knitting at fifteen shillings each week, and if you show promise you might progress to fine knitting.' He consulted a sheet. 'Fine knitting pays seventeen and sixpence.'

Kezzie's eyes brimmed. Seventeen and sixpence! What she could do with seventeen and sixpence! She was going to show the most promise of any person on that whole factory floor.

:

'Thank you again,' she said. She paused. Something had just occurred to her. It was worth a try. Boldness had got her this far already, and she sensed that he was sympathetic.

'Is it possible,' she enquired, 'for me to have an advance against my first pay?'

He stopped with his pen in mid-air and regarded the girl in front of him. He had noted the cheap suit and the make-up, and her feet sliding out of the too large shoes. He was sure that she had tricked herself in first this morning in some way. She was very thin and had a barely concealed desperation about her. But she was also striking-looking and determined and he could see the spirit shining out of her. He might probably never see her or the money again, he thought ruefully.

'I can give you five shillings,' he said, and marked it on her card. 'Give this to Miss Dunlop and she will give you the money and file your card. Congratulations, Miss Munro, you are our very first employee.'

Kezzie stood up. She had to control a sudden urge to run round the other side of the desk and kiss the factory manager on the top of his shiny balding head.

Instead she took her card demurely and went to see the secretary.

She completely forgot to wiggle her bum.

14. A trip to the seaside

Kezzie skipped home like a child out of school. She went to Bella's to tell her the news and give her back her clothes.

'No, no, you keep them,' Bella insisted. 'You've set a standard, now you'll have to keep it up.'

Kezzie stopped at the village shop to get sweets for Lucy, dolly mixtures, aniseed balls and liquorice. She bought tobacco for her grandfather, and for herself a bar of scented soap. As her goods piled up on the counter she sobered up a little and asked for corned beef, condensed milk and some other basics to see them through the week.

Almost immediately there was an incredible change of atmosphere in their caravan. The prospect of a weekly income removed the spectre of starvation which had hovered in their company now for many weeks. Lucy sang as she set the table or washed the dishes. Grandad smiled more often. Kezzie couldn't believe it was all her imagination because she, too, felt as if a burden she had not known she was carrying had been lifted from her shoulders.

Spring came very slowly. The weather was wild for days on end as Kezzie walked to Shawcross and back each day. She didn't mind at all. Wrapped in a huge mackintosh, which had belonged to Bella's husband, Kezzie would willingly have trudged double the distance. She liked the factory. The girls were pleasant and it was good to have company of her own age each day. She was quick and deft at her work and concentrated more than the others, and she soon progressed to the fine knitting, which was easier as you could sit rather than stand. She enjoyed the noise and the bustle even though she was tired with working long hours. She had bought Lucy an almost-new coat and had actually started putting some money away in a savings account.

At the farm the lambing had started and Grandad was getting some work again from the farmer. They were eating better, mince and stews rather than the daily soup and potatoes. Kezzie started to teach Lucy to bake and they had great fun with scones so badly burnt that even the birds would not eat them.

One Thursday night as Kezzie was about to leave work, the manager stopped her.

'Miss Munro,' he said, 'Miss Dunlop's assistant is off ill and we have the wages to make up. Would it be possible for you to wait on?'

Kezzie thought quickly. It would probably mean extra pay, and she could treat herself to a bus ride from Shawcross to the village and not be home any later.

She nodded and took her coat off.

'The floor supervisor says that you are an intelligent girl,' said the manager. 'Have you ever done work like this before?'

'No,' said Kezzie sitting herself down at the table, 'but I –'

'– learn very quickly,' the manager finished for her. They all laughed.

'One day,' he went on, 'you must tell me how you bluffed your way in here first on the interview day.'

Kezzie's face went red and she bent her head and busied herself sealing the wage packets as fast as she could. They finished within an hour or so and he gave her five shillings for overtime. On the way out Miss Dunlop walked with her to the bus stop.

'My assistant is thinking of leaving in the near future. She is to be married in a few months. I wondered if you would be interested in the position? You would require training, but there are classes for shorthand and typing and books you can study. It would be a wonderful opportunity for you.'

A wonderful opportunity, thought Kezzie, on the way home. Yes, it was, and she knew it, but there was faint feeling of disappointment as well. If she trained as a secretary then she was saying farewell to any chance of becoming a doctor. It was ridiculous to hold that dream still. She was being greedy. Not so long ago she had no job and barely enough food, now she was being offered something many would trade places with her for.

She was still unsettled on the day for the works' outing. The firm had hired a bus so that all workers and their families could go. Kezzie was glad to have a day out. It would serve Lucy instead of the annual Sunday school outing. She just could not bear to imagine Lucy, Grandad and herself going on that trip without her father. She had decided that they would be busy with something else that day.

Lucy hardly slept the night before, asking questions every two minutes. How far away is the sea? Will we be on the bus for a long time? Can I make a sandcastle? Eventually Kezzie threatened to leave her behind if she opened her mouth one more time.

The next day everyone made a pet of her. Even the usually austere Miss Dunlop took her on her knee and pointed things out to her through the window as they passed by.

'Your sister is a beautiful child,' she told Kezzie as they all climbed off the bus.

Kezzie looked to where Lucy was running ahead,

pulling Grandad along in her excitement. She *was* very pretty, Kezzie thought, with her blonde curls and blue, blue eyes, but she was still quite thin from the winter, her little body almost frail. And she was so trusting, she would go with anyone, a child unaware of any badness in the world. She must stay that way as long as possible. Time enough for her to come to Kezzie's realisation of the grimness of ordinary existence.

They went on to the sands with their picnics.

'What is it?' asked Lucy in amazement. 'What is it?'

'It's the sea,' said Kezzie, laughing at the wonderment on Lucy's face. 'It's the sea.'

'Come on,' said Grandad. He had taken off his socks and shoes and rolled up his trousers. 'We'll go for a paddle.'

'It keeps moving, Kezzie,' Lucy informed her sister when she came back after about half an hour. 'It moves all the time.'

They had a glorious day. It was warm and sunny and they ate ice-cream and rode on the donkeys, and made sand pies and jumped the waves until they were exhausted. While Grandad and Lucy packed up their things in a bag, Kezzie walked along the beach by herself. Her bare feet sank into the cool sand. The sun was beginning to go down and the sky was green and cream and gold. She breathed in and faced seawards. What was out there, far away where she could not see? Ireland, Michael's home, America, then far far away India and Africa. That was where she was going some day. She would do the secretarial work just now, but she would not give up her dream. She touched her silver locket without knowing it.

On the bus going home they ate chips and the men drank beer. The driver had the headlights on as darkness came down and as they roared along the country roads home, someone started a sing-song. Lucy fell asleep on Grandad's knee.

The bus dropped them at the end of the lane and they carried Lucy home in the gloaming and put her to bed. There was sand in her shoes and in her hair and ears. Kezzie decided she could wait until the morning for a wash.

Grandad made some tea and they sat by the fire drinking it and talking softly.

:

'I think I've spent all our savings,' lamented Kezzie.

'It was worth it,' said her grandfather. 'Did you see the wean's face when I sat her on that donkey and took her for a wee trot around?'

'She must have had about nine rides up and down,' said Kezzie. 'The man was letting her on for nothing at the end. And the ice-cream we ate! Oysters and nougat wafers. No wonder I don't have any money left.'

'Don't you worry too much about the money,' said her grandfather. 'I've got good news for you. I was talking to your manager fellow and he says he might be able to fix me up with a job with a friend of his in Glasgow.'

15. The royal connection

Absolutely nothing, thought Kezzie, could have made her more happy than the expression on her grandfather's face some weeks later when he came back from Glasgow and said: 'I've got a job.'

She had watched him walking down the lane and knew even before he spoke that his news was good. His back seemed straighter and he was swinging his arms.

She brewed some tea as he sat down. Lucy climbed on to his knee and he tucked her into the crook of his arm and began to fill his pipe.

'Come on, tell us,' begged Kezzie.

'It's a proper job,' he said, drawing slowly and making the tobacco glow, 'but I'm not telling you too much about it because I'm planning a wee surprise.'

No matter how much both of them coaxed him in the days which followed he revealed very little. Kezzie knew that he must be at his trade again because he spoke of tools and engineering equipment. She marvelled at the change in him now he felt he had a purpose in life again. His shoulders and arms filled out and there was colour in his face. He was more cheerful both with them and with his cronies whom he had avoided in their bad times. It was so unfair, thought Kezzie, when he needed friends the most he had been ashamed to be seen with threadbare trousers and no money for tobacco or beer.

Finally one weekend, he told them both to get ready as he was taking them to Glasgow.

'Put on your best clothes,' he said. 'I'm taking you to meet royalty.'

Royalty? thought Kezzie as she dressed Lucy with white ankle socks and buckled her new sandals. She remembered Matt McPhee and his mother telling their fortunes.

'There's a royal connection in your life,' she had told her grandfather.

Lucy bounced up and down on the bus seat as they travelled the six or so miles to Glasgow. As the bus entered the city it passed through some very dirty streets with tenement buildings blocking the sun, and ragged children playing in the gutters. Kezzie looked away. She hated to see the children so ill-kempt. It made her uneasy. It must be so much worse, she thought, to be poor in a great city. At least in the country they had fresh air and sunlight.

They went on a tram. For Kezzie and Lucy it was the first time. It made a tremendous noise and seemed to travel at a great speed, although as she watched the houses sliding by she realised they were not going so fast as it appeared. Lucy was scared. She hung on to Grandad as the conductor punched their tickets, rang the bell and called the stops. They passed Queen's Dock and Yorkhill Quay, where the Anchor Line ships came and went across the Atlantic. Through Yoker to Clydebank, past Rothesay Dock and then they stopped at John Brown's shipyard.

:

'The Clyde,' declared Grandad. He pointed to the great grey mass of water which breathed life and hope into workers and their families, a prospect of employment, of pay and food, but more than that, of a pride in something. A job well done, a mission completed, a statement made.

'There she lies,' said Grandad, 'my queen.'

He had taken them through the shipyard gate and they stood a little way off gazing at the huge hull of an ocean-going liner. She was immense. The vastness of her loomed over the little family. The gantries and scaffolding were petty fripperies to be cast aside before her launch. She had a power and a presence that belonged to her alone, a queen indeed.

'I'm on the engineering side of it,' Grandad explained. 'When they got this contract, due to the recession they were actually short of skilled workers. I've got a squad of lads under me. She's due to be launched in the autumn, but even then I'll still be involved in the fitting out.'

He was so proud, Kezzie thought. Proud of his work. Proud of the ship, and of the workers and the skill it took to build something such as this. Only four years before the *Queen Mary*, the first ship over 75,000 tons, had been launched in 1934 from Clydebank. When this one was completed it would be the largest liner in the world. And he was proud of them too, Kezzie realised, as he introduced them to various people he knew on the site.

'My son's bairns,' he said. 'The wee one's awful bonny, and the older one, she's bonny too, but has brains as well. Got herself a good job, good prospects, fine thing for a woman today.'

In the second part of the day they visited the Empire Exhibition at Bellahouston Park in Glasgow. Kezzie had heard about it on the radio in the factory. She had listened with the rest of the girls to the recording of King George VI's speech from Ibrox Park, and the commentary on the royal couple's progress through the Pavilions. According to the reporter, Queen Elizabeth had purchased two Shirley Temple dolls for the little princesses, Elizabeth and Margaret Rose.

Kezzie and Lucy and Grandad got off the tram at Mosspark Boulevard and went through the turnstile.

The exhibition was quite spectacular. They went to the Palace of Engineering first, as this was what Grandad wanted to see. There were models of dams, bridges and ships, as well as domestic appliances.

'Look at that, Kezzie,' said Grandad, 'a machine that can do the washing for you, while you read a magazine.'

'That'll be the day,' Kezzie laughed.

They wandered round the huge park. They saw Canadian Mounties and Red Indians, and a copy of the Victoria Falls in Africa with a model train travelling beneath the water. Lucy was fascinated with the fountains, she kept running to trail her fingers in the water. They stopped at the bandstand and sat on the green folding chairs where they could listen to the music while eating lunch. Grandad made Lucy a paper boat and she went to sail it in the lake. Kezzie looked around her. The music was playing a lively march and there seemed to her to be a lot of smartly dressed people about chatting and smiling.

'Do you think things are getting better?' she asked her grandfather. 'Maybe folk have more work now, with all this building.'

:

'I don't know,' he said. 'Rearmament's a false salvation, whether you agree with war or not. The world's changing and Scotland's not keeping up. Engineering skills and tools will have to progress or we'll slump again. I suppose that conditions will improve as the government places defence contracts, but what a price to pay for employment. War will come, unless someone sorts that bully out in his own back yard, and then . . .'

Kezzie shivered in the sun. She didn't like to think about war. It was only twenty years since the last one had ended. Her grandad rarely spoke of it. A carnage, she had heard him say once. War didn't belong here, with mothers pushing prams and couples strolling hand in hand, and the sound of children's excited screams from the amusement park. Earlier they had visited the Peace Pavilion. Perhaps it was significant that it was a small wooden building tucked away from the main exhibition.

They collected Lucy from the lake and spent the rest of the afternoon in the Amusement Park. They saw Indian dancers and a magician and persuaded Grandad to have a ride on the mountain switchback railway. When they came out it was dark. The fountains were still playing but were floodlit in changing colours of red, blue, green and yellow. They could see the coloured cascades running down either side of the hill. Above it all, like a beacon of hope, rose Tait's Tower, the Tower of Empire. The silverised steel shaft glittered in the brilliant floodlights and its three observation balconies were edged with red, green and yellow light.

It was an unforgettable sight and they gazed at it for many minutes before turning for home.

16. The accident

Kezzie adapted to working in the factory office very well and Miss Dunlop was pleased with her. She had a good memory and more and more she was being left to work on her own. The firm had an insurance scheme for non-manual workers and as the money was taken from her wages each week before she received them, Kezzie hardly noticed the loss. Because of this, and Grandad's steady employment, Kezzie had peace of mind and for the first time in a long while she felt safe.

As their fortunes improved and the summer faded she and Grandad began to discuss leaving the caravan and finding better accommodation for the winter.

'We could try for one of these new houses the council are building just outside Shawcross,' said Grandad. 'Now that we're on regular wages we would manage the rent.'

Grandad was obviously well thought of in the shipyard – respected by men and managers alike. The foreman had called him aside one day and enquired if he would be willing to travel to Edinburgh with a group of other workers for a special job the following week.

'We'll wait until you come back before looking for a house,' said Kezzie as she saw him off at the bus station in Shawcross. She would be sorry to leave the caravan with its cosy familiarity but the thought of living in a house again with proper washing facilities and space to move about in appealed to her.

It was Friday and as she finished work with her pay in her pocket she felt light-hearted at the prospect of a weekend with just her and Lucy in the caravan. She would take the bus tonight, she decided. It would be quicker, then they would have time to do some baking.

They could go for a walk and pick flowers and maybe stay up late and make toast by the fire. Sunday, they would visit Bella who was laid up with 'flu.

There was light drizzle falling as she boarded the bus, not enough to dampen Kezzie's spirits, but just as much, she realised later, to make the roads slippery and dangerous. It was a single-decker. She sat at the front and wrote a shopping list for tomorrow.

She looked up as the bus approached the crossroads at the edge of the town. Kezzie heard the driver curse. Crossing slowly, and directly in front of them, was a dray pulled by a Clydesdale. Kezzie gasped and gripped her seat as the driver braked hard. On the wet road the bus skidded and the last thing Kezzie could recall was the red brick wall which came rushing towards her.

Lucy had walked to the end of the lane and back hundreds of times, she thought. She was hungry and it was getting cooler and still Kezzie did not come. It was going to be special tonight, Kezzie had promised her, with Grandad away. Lucy had changed into her old clothes, greased the griddle and set the table and washed her hands twice, and still Kezzie was not home.

She looked up and down the road and then very cautiously stepped out into the middle. She was forbidden to go any further than the end of the lane on her own, but would it do any harm to walk just a little way along and see if she could spot Kezzie coming? She made up her mind to go. After all, when she met Kezzie she could help carry the shopping. She ran back to put on her coat and taking her doll for company she set off down the road.

'Is it right or left?' Lucy asked her doll as they reached the road junction. She gazed up at the signpost. The black letters were all worn away with the wind and rain and anyway one of the arms pointed into a field. 'That's silly, isn't it?' said Lucy. She lifted her doll so that its mouth was at her ear and pretended to listen to what it was saying. Then with great determination she started down the road on the left. Behind her the signpost pointed the way to Glasgow.

She HAD to meet Kezzie on the road, she told the doll firmly, after she had walked a few miles. There was no other way to go. She held the doll up in her arms so that she would be able to see Kezzie first. After another twenty minutes or so her arms got tired and she tucked the doll inside her coat and buttoned it up. A breakdown van towing a bus with a smashed windscreen passed her slowly. The driver called to her: 'Are you all right, little girl?'

'Yes,' said Lucy. 'I'm going to meet my sister.'

The man waved and drove on.

Eventually Lucy saw a scattering of houses on the road. She had no sense of how far she had come or indeed where she was, only a fixed idea in her mind that if she kept on walking she would meet Kezzie. Perhaps she could ask at one of the houses if anyone had seen her sister. As she approached a big black and tan dog ran at her and started barking. She hurried off, further into the city. Very soon she was completely lost and although she had decided to walk back to the caravan she did not know which road to take. It was getting dark and the streets where she wandered became mean and dingy. She sat down on the edge of a pavement and tried hard not to cry.

'Are you lost, hen?' A wheezing voice asked.

Lucy looked up. An old woman with a black shawl was bending over her. She was very smelly, Lucy thought, and didn't appear to have any teeth at all. Lucy would normally have found this quite funny but at the moment she was too concerned with her sore legs and empty stomach.

She hesitated. She shouldn't speak to someone she did not know, but there was no one else about.

'A little bit,' she admitted.

'Aw, ma poor wee lamb,' the old woman sat down beside her and began to finger Lucy's coat. 'That's a lovely coat you've got on,' she said, 'but I can see it's a wee bittie too small for you. Would you like a new one?'

Lucy looked at the sleeves on her coat. It *was* getting too small for her now, but she hadn't dared mention it to Kezzie because she had already had a new cardigan and skirt for going back to school. Was it greedy to want so much?

'And yer boots,' the woman was untying the laces carefully, 'are yer wee toes pinched in them boots?'

Lucy nodded.

'I thought as much,' said the woman gently, 'you

just slip them off and hand them to me. There's a shop at the end of the road where they change things for ye.'

Lucy hesitated.

'Here's a barley sugar for ye tae suck while yer waiting,' the woman wheedled.

That decided it. By this time Lucy was very hungry. She grasped the barley-sugar stick in one hand and with her doll in the other, sat down to wait for the old lady's return from this magic shop where you could get new clothes for old ones.

An hour passed and it became very dark and Lucy realised slowly that the old woman was not coming back. There were people passing by staring at her, rough people who shouted and swore. She got up and stumbled on.

It was very late and the pubs were emptying their last regulars into the streets. She paused outside one as the door swung open and jammed. She could see lights and warmth and she wanted more than anything to be back in her own home. A man came towards her with a bottle in his hand.

'Hallo, pet,' he asked kindly. 'Are ye waitin' for yer da?'

'My daddy's dead,' said Lucy.

'That's a shame, yer ma then?'

'She's dead too,' said Lucy sadly.

The man burst into tears. Lucy stared at him. She had never seen a man crying before.

'That's a terrible shame,' he sobbed. He took a drink from his bottle and then handed it to her. 'Here,' he offered generously, 'this'll cheer ye up.'

Lucy drank some of the tea-coloured liquid. It burned her throat, but quite soon she did feel better.

'Would you help me find my way home?' she asked him.

'Certainly,' he waved his arms about. 'Just point me in the right direction. I can always find my way home.'

'I don't know the direction,' said Lucy, her voice wavering.

The man put his arm around her shoulder. 'Come over here and sit down and tell me how you got here, and then we'll work out how to get back.'

The two of them sat down with their backs to the

pub wall. Lucy sipped some more of the cold tea, and told the man her story. When she had finished she turned to ask him to take her home. He was fast asleep!

She stood up, uncertain what to do next. Maybe he wasn't well and she should ask someone for help. She herself was beginning to feel very unwell. She staggered down the road, trailing her doll by one arm.

17. Where is Lucy?

Kezzie was walking in fog. It drifted and swirled about her and she couldn't see in front of her at all. She must sit down and rest. She was very tired. Her head ached so badly and she knew that there was something important which she must remember. There were reports to file, and order forms to make up. Miss Dunlop would be cross with her if she did not finish them.

Miss Dunlop *was* cross with Kezzie, very cross indeed.

'This is the third day she has not turned up for work,' she snapped at the manager. 'These young people have no sense of responsibility. I trained up that other girl then she decides to get married, and now this . . .'

The manager tapped his pen slowly on the edge of the desk.

'It's not like her, you know, not Miss Munro. Even if she was ill I would have thought she would have sent a note.' He paused. 'I think I'll give the shipyard where her grandfather works a ring and enquire.'

Fifteen minutes later he came through to Miss Dunlop's desk.

'They say he's gone to the east coast for a week's work, and as far as they know the girls were fine when he left. They say he's always talking about them so they're sure he would have mentioned if they'd been ill.'

They both looked at each other.

'We'll take a run out to where she lives in your car after work tonight,' said Miss Dunlop briskly, 'and find out what's what.'

Far from finding out what was what, their visit to the caravan only worried them further. The door was ajar, the table set for tea but the fire was out and the place was cold.

'The police station, I think,' said Miss Dunlop, pulling on her gloves. Her hands shook a little. She would never have admitted it but she had developed a real fondness for Kezzie, and was now very concerned that something quite awful had happened to her and the child.

An hour later they were in the cottage hospital.

'We had no means of identifying her,' the doctor told them, 'and no one came forward to report her missing. Any bag which she may have been carrying was not recovered from the wreck. She's actually lucky to be alive.'

'Is she very bad?' asked Miss Dunlop, gripping her bag tightly.

'It's hard to say. She's severely concussed. She could be that way for months, or wake up tomorrow.'

Miss Dunlop came out of the hospital with the factory manager. She stopped with her hand on the handle of the car door.

'Where,' she said, 'I wonder, is Lucy?'

'LUCY,' repeated the lady in the white starched apron.

She wrote it in the orphanage register. She smiled at the small waif with the stained clothes and tangled hair in front of her. 'And you can't remember your second name?'

Lucy shook her head. She couldn't remember anything at this moment. It had taken an hour of coaxing to get her to say her first name. She couldn't remember how she got here or where her coat and shoes were. The policeman, who had found her wandering drunk beside the river at three o'clock in the morning, had never seen such a terrified child before.

Her mother and father were both dead, at least they had established that, and she had obviously been deliberately abandoned by whoever was supposed to be looking after her. It was a disgrace, thought the nurse. Children always suffered the most in a depression. She would have to give her a second name. She recalled where they had found the child. 'Clyde', she added in the book.

'Come on now, Lucy Clyde,' she said gently, 'and we'll give you a nice bath and some warm soup.'

'You've got room for her then,' said the policeman,

:

glad that the problem was now someone else's.

'Actually, we haven't,' said the matron. 'We're full to bursting. But there's a group of orphans being emigrated to Canada at the end of the week, and if she's not claimed by then we might manage to squeeze her in.'

'Where in Canada do they go?' asked the policeman.

'All over,' said the matron. 'They are sent to Receiving Houses in various places and then placed in good homes. I've had letters from there, and Australia and New Zealand. Lots of children now have whole new families, and are enjoying open spaces and sunshine.'

'Wish it was me,' said the policeman, snapping shut his notebook.

Miss Dunlop visited Kezzie in the hospital the next day. Kezzie's grandfather arrived as she sat by the bedside. She spoke to him of her concern for Lucy.

'Don't worry,' he said, 'Aunt Bella will have her.' He placed his hand on Kezzie's forehead. 'Come on now, Kezzie,' he said, 'you've slept long enough.'

Kezzie could feel the mist clearing slowly from around her. She felt warmer. The sun must be shining and, better still, her headache was less severe. She opened her eyes. It was very bright, and she was not outside as she had imagined but in a room lying down in bed. Her grandad was there, and Miss Dunlop. She wanted to laugh, they looked so serious. She smiled at them.

'I'm all right,' she said. Then she remembered her dream and the thing she had been trying so hard to recall. 'Is Lucy with you, Grandad?'

Kezzie became like a person demented. She discharged herself from the hospital immediately, despite the doctor's dire warnings. When she eventually realised that Lucy had not been seen for days her distress was profound. They went from house to house in the village and then started a search of Shawcross.

'A child that age, wandering off,' said the sergeant at the police station, 'anything could happen to her. She could fall in a burn or go away across the peats. We might never find her.'

Kezzie clenched her fists and tried not to scream. It

was all she could do to control herself. She felt like running up and down the streets shouting wildly.

'Or the tinkers,' the sergeant went on, 'taking a child's the sort of thing they would do.'

'They would NEVER do something like that,' said Kezzie angrily. She was just about to say something very rude when her grandfather came running in.

'One of the bus drivers at the garage saw a little girl walking on the road to Glasgow last Friday. She told him she was going to meet her sister.'

'Glasgow!' cried Kezzie. 'Glasgow!'

'She must have taken the wrong turn at the road end,' said Grandad. He turned to the sergeant. 'Can you check with the Glasgow police, if any child has turned up there?'

By evening they were speaking to the matron of the children's home.

'I don't understand how you can do something like that.' Kezzie was in tears. 'She's halfway to Canada with a different name and her own family don't know.'

'To us she was an abandoned child,' said the matron

defensively. 'Lots of children have been sent out over the years. Very few go now, but it gave many a good start in life. We have letters from them telling us how well their new families treat them. We were doing it for the best.'

'If I get a passage right away,' said Kezzie as she and Grandad walked down the high street, 'I'll only be days behind her when she lands and I should catch up with her easily enough over there.'

'It's a big country,' said her grandad doubtfully. 'You can't go alone.'

Kezzie turned to face him among the crowds of people which, as always in cities, seemed to be hurrying by.

'Grandad, you know that I have to go. There is no other way to be absolutely sure of bringing her back. She will be terrified and she needs me with her as quickly as possible.' Kezzie stopped, her eyes brimming with tears. 'You also know,' she went on, 'that it's best you stay here and keep on your job, for us to have something to come back to.' They walked on in silence.

Kezzie pawned everything she had, and gave the tickets to Bella. It didn't come to much, she thought, as she counted the money into her purse. She would need every penny, not just for her passage, but also for whatever travelling she might have to do in Canada. So, she only hesitated for a second when the pawnbroker, eyeing her carefully, said, 'I'll give you two and six for that silver locket you're wearing.'

'Three shillings,' said Kezzie, unfastening it and placing it on the counter.

The factory had a collection which the manager and Miss Dunlop made up to fifty pounds. Kezzie was speechless.

'I can't guarantee you the same position when you return,' said the manager, 'but you'll get the first vacancy on the floor.'

At the dockside her grandad kept wiping his face with his handkerchief as they said goodbye.

Eventually Kezzie said, 'Grandad, I'm going aboard now, and I'm going below deck so don't stay to wave me off.'

They kissed and hugged each other and as they

separated Kezzie saw, striding towards her, the tall dark figure of Michael Donohoe.

He wrapped his arms around her.

'I went to visit you all, and I met Bella who told me of your misfortune. Kezzie, I wish I was going with you.'

'Why don't you?' asked Kezzie. 'You said you wanted to emigrate.'

He avoided her gaze for a moment.

'Things did not go as well as I had hoped in London . . . and, well, I've joined up.'

'The army?' Kezzie was aghast.

He shrugged. 'There's a war coming, and it's regular pay with meals.'

The ship's hooter sounded. Kezzie lifted her case.

'I've something for you,' said Michael quickly. 'Some sandwiches.' He pushed a brown paper parcel into her bag. 'And . . . I got one of your Colleen Bawn tickets from Bella.' He opened his fist and in it lay Kezzie's locket.

Kezzie drew her breath in.

'Michael,' she said softly.

He shifted his feet uncomfortably. 'Now, you be sure and find her,' he said.

'Oh, I shall find her,' said Kezzie. 'I shall cross the sea and travel the land until I do. I shall search all Canada for her. In every town and village I shall look for her. And I *will* find her,' she stopped and then went on, 'and when I have, then I will bring her home.'

Part II

CANADA

18. A game of chess

Lucy thought she had died and gone to a bad place. She had not been good enough for the angels to take her to Mummy and Daddy in heaven. She was in a little wooden coffin with a lid which she could reach up above her head and touch, and it kept heaving up and down, up and down. She gripped her dolly desperately. She was going to be sick.

Kezzie waited until they had left the Tail o' the Bank before she opened Michael's brown paper parcel. She should have known, she thought, as she gazed at the money. Ten and five pound notes spilled on to her lap. There was a note laboriously scribed by someone not accustomed to writing letters.

'My Dear Kezzie please take this money to find Lucy and do not be so proud as not to use it. Who knows what might happen on the other side of the water. Money opens doors. I know this and I also know I love you. Your friend Michael.'

Kezzie saw the horizon through a blur of tears. She stayed on deck a long time and watched Scotland growing smaller and the sun setting before going to her cabin.

The next day was calm and beautiful and people strolled about on deck. Kezzie spoke to no one. She had cried herself to sleep last night, with the thought of Lucy, travelling steerage, frightened and alone. She could not cope with company just now, and was not inclined to make idle chat. She waited until the dining-room was almost empty before taking her meals, and always sought the most isolated part of the ship to sit with her book and read. She was not the only person doing this, she noticed after several days. A young man with sandy hair and the beginnings of a moustache often came last to eat, usually accompanied by an older woman. It was not difficult to notice also that he walked with a limp – an iron calliper clamped his left leg just below the knee of his plus-fours and reached to his ankle. He took to nodding across to Kezzie each day and finally she conceded his presence with a small wave.

The sea was rougher and the waves higher as the days passed and autumn came with cold rain which lashed the deck and sent most people below. Eventually even Kezzie gave up and entered the small non-smoking lounge with her rain-soaked book in her hand. Her friend from the dining-room was sitting at a table playing himself at chess. The lady was doing some crochet. Kezzie studied his game from her seat a little way off. As he reached to move the white bishop she drew in her breath. He looked up quickly.

'Do you play?' he asked in surprise.

'Why not?' asked Kezzie at once.

'Why not indeed?' he laughed. 'Would you play me?'

:

The woman looked over with a slight frown on her face.

'Sorry, I should have introduced us. This is my mother, Mrs Fitzwilliam, and I am William James Fitzwilliam.'

Kezzie held out her hand.

'I am Kezzie Munro, from Stonevale,' she said.

The older woman hesitated for the smallest second before taking her hand.

'My husband is Sir Gerald Fitzwilliam,' she said distinctly, 'from Close Manor near Derby.'

Lady Fitzwilliam then detached her hand from Kezzie's and took up her crochet.

'What kind of name is Kezzie, my dear?' she enquired very politely, after a moment.

Kezzie felt slightly crushed, as this woman had no doubt intended, she thought. She could feel her face redden and her temper rise.

'It is a Biblical name,' she replied, equally courteously. 'Keziah was one of the daughters of Job, if you are familiar with that story.'

'Oh, well played, Kezzie!' cried William enthusiastically. 'I knew when I first spotted you that you had a fine spirit. Just ignore Ma,' he went on, 'she is a dreadful old snob. I am trying to educate her out of it.' He patted his mother affectionately on the head and took his place again at the table.

Kezzie was appalled at such cheek and looked anxiously at Lady Fitzwilliam. To her surprise she was smiling.

'You are an impertinent young man,' she said fondly to her son. She turned to Kezzie. 'One has to be very careful these days, especially on Atlantic crossings. All sorts of people travel abroad now.'

William laughed again.

'See what I mean?' he said. 'She probably suspects you of being a "New Woman". You don't smoke or drink or drive a car or anything?'

'No,' said Kezzie.

'Drat!' said William, snapping his fingers. 'I've been waiting all my life to meet a fast woman.'

'William James!' cried his mother. 'Don't use such language.'

'OK, OK,' he replied. 'Now,' he said to Kezzie, 'shall I take a handicap?'

:

'Whatever for?' said Kezzie, as she arranged the pieces on the board.

Three hours later they agreed on a draw. Thank you, Grandad, Kezzie said silently as they went into dinner.

William was cheerful and kind and as the weather worsened and his mother stayed more in her cabin, the two of them walked the decks together, or played chess in the lounge. She told him of her mission and he explained that they were travelling to America via Canada to seek treatment for his leg which was wasting below the knee.

Kezzie viewed the heavy iron brace with distaste.

'Do you need that thing on all the time?' she asked him one day. 'It must weigh you down and surely prevent development. Perhaps if you removed it from time to time and exercised your muscles, it would help.'

'You are a very clever girl,' he replied, 'and if you promise not to tell Ma I'll let you into a secret.' He showed her the top of the caliper. 'I got the village blacksmith to fit this like so,' and with a little tap the brace fell apart. 'Now, I have been doing exercises to build up my strength, but Ma would have a fit. She thinks I would collapse completely if this contraption was removed.'

It was the sort of thing that would have intrigued Grandad, thought Kezzie, as William put the parts together again. Anything requiring skill in metalwork interested him. Grandad . . . he seemed so far away, Scotland and Stonevale, and Bella and the rest.

A week passed and Kezzie was grateful for William's company. He seemed to sense when she needed time by herself to think, and when she was low his bright conversations cheered her immensely.

One morning she was awakened early by the sound of the ship's foghorn. She dressed warmly and went on deck. A dense white fog surrounded the ship. The foghorn sounded again mournfully, as the ship moved slowly forward.

'We're nearing Newfoundland,' said William appearing beside her, rubbing his hands together.

The fog swirled eerily obscuring sea and sky and deadening sound.

'Look!' said Kezzie.

A massive shape half-hidden in the mist loomed beside the ship.

'An iceberg!' said William.

They heard the sailors call immediately, and the foghorn sounded once more. They continued their slow progress as the iceberg made its stately departure off the starboard bow. It was a magnificent sight and the sense of danger seemed to thrill William. Kezzie fretted all day, aware of the time she was losing.

At last they entered the Gulf of St Lawrence and she calmed herself. Now she could actually see Canada. They would sail up the St Lawrence River tomorrow, and then her search would really begin.

19. Lucy arrives in Canada

The ship Lucy was in had fared much worse in the crossing. It had pitched and rolled and Lucy had retched so much that she didn't care any more about being made to go to sleep in a coffin. On the few occasions she had been taken on deck she had been very frightened. Why was there water all around? Where was the beach, with sand and the donkeys? Far out at sea the movement of the boat on the surface of the ocean was unlike anything Lucy had ever experienced before. These were not the gentle waters that had lapped around her ankles when she had splashed on the shoreline on the summer outing. The water was grey and roaring and angry. It slid past the rails and heaved the deck about so that she could scarcely keep her balance as the ship tilted and dipped.

The lady who was in charge of them was seasick for most of the journey, and the older children, who were supposed to look after Lucy, teased and made fun of her. One boy, in particular, pushed into her at meal-times and stole her food.

She was frightened of the sailors who tried to be kind to her. They spoke with words she did not know and they had strange red and blue drawings on their arms.

As they neared the coast the ship was trapped in pack ice for several days, moving forward slowly by degrees as the crew tried to keep the propellors free. The bitter cold was something she was not used to. Her clothes were thin and inadequate and she shivered hopelessly. It was a distressed sick little girl who disembarked from the ship in Canada.

As they filed into the huge Immigration shed Lucy was aware of only one thing. Although she had no idea where in the world she was, she knew she was very far away from her grandad, Kezzie and their snug caravan.

Alexander Dalgleish had been processing immigrants for many years now. As he surveyed the long shambling queue of people it seemed to him that on some days every nation on earth filed past him. He rubbed the back of his neck and eased his aching muscles. It would soon be the weekend. He would get away out of the crowded city to his cabin deep in the pine woods. A little fishing and a trek in the forest under the stars and he would feel better. It must be in the blood, he thought. His grandfather had been one of the original Nor'Westers, who had opened up the vast track of the Canadian Shield. Forced to quit Scotland he had arrived in the unknown continent and become one of the fur traders that had paddled and portaged their way up rivers and across lakes to map out the Canadian interior. Explorers, whose adventuring spirit had chartered waterfalls and mountains and left as their legacy their names on maps for ever. He felt that this inheritance was what had made Canada the way it was.

:

A vibrant nation, a people more at ease outdoors, dynamic and friendly.

And now? The Old World and the New World merged before him. New hopefuls arriving on every ship, with talent to offer and a prospect of a chance to use it.

He frowned as he caught sight of the group of children. The Great Depression had lessened the welcoming attitude to immigrants as people were afraid there would not be so much for native-born Canadians. Also, Canadian law had been tightened up over the last few years, with different regulations being passed in order to protect the welfare of child immigrants. Still, it might be a better life here for some of the poor waifs he had seen. Some sun and good farm feeding would give them a new start in life.

When the children cleared Immigration they joined up with another group who had come in on a Liverpool ship. There was a quick conference between the two women who were escorting the children.

'They have to be regrouped and sent to different places,' said the Liverpool escort.

'I must spend the night here and then go to

Carrville at the Lakes,' said the woman who had been with Lucy's group. 'And I am heartily glad, I can tell you. I was ill, absolutely ill, on that dreadful boat.'

The other woman consulted her papers. 'I don't believe it! All the way to British Columbia, and the train's due to leave.' She looked around her crossly. 'Where are they? Right, gather up your belongings,' she snapped at the children.

The women sorted out the certificates and papers.

'Hurry UP,' comanded the woman who was now Lucy's escort, 'or we'll miss the train.'

A train? Lucy thought she would only get more lost if she went on a train. She knew that she was being taken further and further away from where she belonged. Crowds of people moved all about her and made her dizzy and more confused. If only she could think for a minute and decide what to do. She sat down on her little cardboard suitcase and sat her doll beside her. She would stay here and wait. That was it! If she stayed still in one place for a while she would stop being lost. It might take a little time, but Kezzie and Grandad would find her.

'Get up,' said an angry voice.

Lucy shook her head firmly. Kezzie MUST be looking for her, she had been lost a long time. If she could remain in one place then it would make it easy for Kezzie to come and collect her.

The next moment Lucy was slapped on the side of the head so hard that she was knocked across her suitcase and on to the ground. Never in her life before had she been treated so roughly. Even when she had been very naughty she had only been smacked on the hand.

'When I tell you to do something, you do it.'

Lucy got slowly to her feet, utterly stunned. She put her hands to her ringing head. The woman grabbed her arm and shook her.

'Is there something the matter with you?'

Lucy stared at her, unseeing.

'Is this child dumb or what?' the woman asked of no one in particular.

'Yeh,' said the boy who had taken Lucy's food on the ship, 'she's real dumb.'

'Why do I always get the worst ones?' moaned the

woman. She picked up Lucy's case and as she did so, the rag doll fell unnoticed to the ground, she took Lucy roughly by the hand. 'Follow me, all of you,' she ordered, 'and stay together.'

Alexander Dalgleish stared after them. He had seen many sights in his years in the Immigration sheds but for callous cruelty that one took some beating. He shook his head and, as he moved forward to deal with the next person in line, he noticed something lying on the stone floor. He gazed for a moment at the small crumpled object with its tangled woollen hair which lay with one arm outstretched. He turned away. Then he glanced back again.

He hesitated for a second, then he vaulted the bench, scooped up Lucy's doll and ran after the forlorn little group.

20. William's accident

Kezzie could see the Canadian Red Ensign fluttering beside the Union Jack on the top of the biggest building in the harbour. She and William were right forward on the ship watching the sailors unloading from the hold. Her first impressions of the country were the huge scale of everything, and the amount of people moving about the dockside. There seemed to be a vast amount of ships of every nationality loading and unloading.

'Hold on,' said William, 'I'm going to take your picture.' He ducked under the barrier and walked backwards with his Box Brownie camera in his hand.

∴

'Don't go too far up there, William,' called his mother who was standing a little way behind Kezzie.

'Don't fuss, Ma,' he called back. 'I'm miles away from the hold.'

He indicated the open hatch several feet away from him, and bent his head to look in the viewfinder.

What happened next took only seconds but to Kezzie it was like a drama played out before her eyes in slow motion. The load from the hold swung across high above them and, as the black shadow of it passed between her and William, something detached itself from the netting and fell.

'Smile please,' cried William. Then he was struck on the back of the neck, spun round and toppled over the side.

Kezzie reached out automatically with her hands, as she heard William's mother scream. She looked round for help. Lady Fitzwilliam had fainted. No one else had seen what had happened. Kezzie ran to the side and stared at the water. It was black and oily. There was no sign of him, only his cloth cap floating on the surface. He might be unconscious. And then she thought of something else. With that calliper on his leg he would sink like a stone.

She dragged off her jacket and skirt and aiming at the spot where she guessed he had gone down she dived from the rail.

Kezzie had learned to swim, as all the village children had, in the local river and canal. This water was different. It was much colder, deeper and darker. She reckoned she had one chance. If she didn't locate him the first time it would be too late. William, manacled in iron, would sink quickly. So she dived as deeply as she could, groping blindly with her hands at anything.

Her lungs were bursting and her heart was thudding. She would have to go up. She struck out wildly around her and, grabbing to the side, found the rough cloth of a tweed jacket. She had him!

He was a dead weight. She couldn't pull him up at all. In fact he was pulling her down. She manoeuvred herself under his body, and felt for the caliper. With the ends of her breath releasing into the icy water she battered the clip. It fell away and at once he started to rise.

There were coloured lights in her head, and though by now she had a firm grip on his belt, she felt herself weaken. Water trickled into the side of her mouth. She looked up, no light above. She was failing and she knew it. It had been too late – for both of them. Time drifted . . . It would have been like this in the pit, she thought . . . black . . . nothing. She closed her eyes and in the double darkness she could hear her father . . . softly . . . 'Kezzie'.

With the little strength she had left she kicked for the surface.

Two sailors were in the water beside them and she felt herself being lifted and William being taken from her. Then she was violently sick in the bottom of a rowing boat.

On Lady Fitzwilliam's instructions they were taken to a private clinic and despite Kezzie's protests she was put to bed and made to rest. Lady Fitzwilliam entered her room a few hours later.

The older woman came and at once placed her hands over Kezzie's.

'My dear child,' she said, 'you are intelligent enough

to know what William means to me. He is dearer to me than life itself. If I can ever be of assistance to you, you must tell me.'

'I need help now,' replied Kezzie. 'I must leave here at once, I have lost time already and I am so worried about my sister.'

'I know,' said Lady Fitzwilliam. 'I have already made enquiries on your behalf. I went to the Receiving Home here and have discovered that a party of children stayed there and then were sent on to Carrville, near the American border.'

'Can we be sure that it is the right group?' asked Kezzie.

Lady Fitzwilliam smiled triumphantly.

'I'm afraid I may have bullied them just a little,' she said.

Kezzie could imagine that only too well.

'At any rate I persuaded them to allow me to see their records. One of the children was called Lucy Clyde!'

'Lucy!' said Kezzie. She was close to Lucy.

'How do I get to Carrville?' she asked.

Lady Fitzwilliam opened her bag and took out

some documents. 'I have that in hand for you. This is an aeroplane ticket which I booked on your behalf. I thought it would be much quicker than travelling by train. Also, here is a letter of recommendation,' she went on. 'It may ease your way with officials. My husband is slightly acquainted with John Buchan, the governor general. He is a Scot, you know.'

'Yes,' said Kezzie.

She packed her suitcase. William's mother had sensed that to give her money would have been insulting but had insisted on buying Kezzie some new clothes to replace those ruined in the river.

William was to stay at the clinic for a few days until the cut on his head healed. Kezzie's goodbye to William saddened her. He had become a cheerful friend which she had badly needed.

'I want you to have this.' He took a fountain pen from his pocket. 'I would like you to have something which belonged to me to remember me by.'

They looked at each other.

'I will write to you,' said Kezzie reassuringly. 'And you have my aunt's address. And your leg *will* get better.'

:

'If you say it will, then I believe it.' He gripped her by the shoulders. 'Good luck, Kezzie,' he said. 'Dear Kezzie, the bravest and the best.'

21. Niagara Falls

When Kezzie arrived at the airfield she stared hard at the aeroplane which was to take her down to Carrville. She knew that it was thirty-odd years since two American brothers had managed to get a power-driven machine into the sky and that many advances had been made since then. But the appearance of the plane itself, when viewed up close, did not inspire confidence. One could see the joins quite clearly on the pieces of metal and the wings seemed too fragile to hold together once the engine started, and yet at the same time too heavy to allow the plane to stay airborne.

As she climbed the stair trolley to board the aircraft Kezzie remembered how daunted she had been when boarding ship in Glasgow to sail across the Atlantic. Now that seemed a minor adventure compared with actually allowing yourself to be lifted up into the air to a great height, and remain there with nothing at all above, around or below you.

She settled herself in her seat and pulled back the little curtain to look out of the porthole. She swallowed nervously. The ground seemed far enough away already and they weren't even airborne!

The engines were switched on, and a tremendous roar filled the cabin. The plane began to shudder. Kezzie closed her eyes and gripped the arms of her seat.

'You all right, honey?' said a voice beside her.

Kezzie opened her eyes. A little old lady had taken the seat on her left.

Kezzie gave a brief smile, and then her eyes opened wider as the plane began to move forward rather bumpily towards the runway.

'First time flying, isn't it? I thought so,' said the lady who introduced herself as Janine le Pointe. 'Going down to see my folks at the lakes. Flown dozens of times myself.' She rummaged in her handbag and brought out a bag of barley sugar sweets. 'Here suck on one of these,' she advised.

Kezzie did as she was told and as the plane rolled faster and faster along the grass she managed one more quick peek out of the window. She gasped at what she saw. They had taken off! She, Kezzie Munro from Stonevale in Scotland, was flying in the skies above the continent of the Americas.

The plane twitched and dipped, pulled by the air currents, and then the pilot set its nose up and they climbed higher. Suddenly they were above the clouds. Despite her fear Kezzie could not stop gazing out of the window. A rumpled white carpet of cloud lay below them, and the sun shone in a sky of the clearest blue she had ever seen.

'It's unbelievable,' said Kezzie, speaking louder above the noise of the engines.

Her companion nodded.

'I always get the same thrill, every time I go up,' said Janine. 'Look now.' She pointed down where the mass of white clouds were drifting apart and they could see below them a thick forest of spruce trees with many little mirrors of lakes reflecting back at them.

They flew over checker-board fields with small farms and churches picked out in white clapboard. The city of Ottawa lay to their right as the plane headed south following the line of the St Lawrence River. The clear water flashed many feet below them. Kezzie could see the river busy with boats on this main trade artery of both Canada and America.

Janine chatted to her, telling her all about her family. She was a French Canadian, who had lived in Montreal all her life. Her son had married and gone to live near the shores of Lake Erie to grow grapes and produce wine.

'His wine is the best in all Canada. It has the taste of summer and the sun. We are still very French,' she said proudly.

As the plane reached the outskirts of Toronto the pilot swung away to the left, out over Lake Ontario.

'Ah,' said Janine. 'I'd hoped he would do this. Not all of the pilots do. Now,' she instructed Kezzie, 'do not take your eyes from the window for a single second.'

Kezzie sat up and did as she was told and several moments later saw a view which was to remain with her to the end of her days.

The great tumbling falls of Niagara were suddenly in her sight. A tremendous natural waterfall, cascading, never-ending, glittering water. Far below she could see the *Maid of the Mists* boats cruising as close as they dared, with the tourists' upturned faces. What could man create which could equal this? A shroud of mist hung over the waterfall and a wraith of a rainbow hung suspended between earth and heaven.

Kezzie gasped.

' "Ontario" is a word from the Iroquois,' said Janine in her ear. 'It means, "beautiful water".'

Kezzie could well understand why the Indians had named this place with such words. The tiny plane swept over the abrupt drop and Kezzie could see the emerald waters foaming below her.

'The water is green because of the mineral deposits,' Janine went on. 'Many lakes in Canada are this beautiful colour. In the wintertime the Falls are quite spectacular. The spray remains frozen on the surrounding trees, and the whole area has a magical look about it.'

When they landed Janine led Kezzie quickly and efficiently through the terminal building. For all her small size she was a woman who commanded attention. They shared a cab into the town, passing fruit and vegetable sellers with their goods in huge baskets by the roadside.

'You'll find lots of the people hereabouts are French or Scots,' said Janine. 'The type of work available in Canada seemed to suit Scottish people in particular, farming and fishing. The big new addition to the power house at the Falls was dug out of the cliff face by men from the Isle of Lewis. It was very hard and dangerous work. Of course a lot go over to the States because the money is better and there's work in the car factories in Detroit.'

Kezzie remembered Janine on the plane pointing out the United States of America, just a few moments away from them. She thought suddenly of Michael, who had given up his chance of emigrating by giving her all his savings. A sudden pang of homesickness took hold of her.

'I'm sorry I can't be of more help,' the older woman said when they reached the station, 'but I've a train to make.' She patted Kezzie on the cheek. 'Don't look so worried, honey. I was a school teacher for forty years, and I reckon I'm a good judge of character. You are a young lady with a very strong sense of purpose. I just *know* you'll find her.'

An hour or so later when Kezzie was sitting in the supervisor's office in the Rescue Home at Carrville she tried to make herself have the same conviction.

Seeing the stunned expression on the girl's face before him the supervisor repeated what he had said slowly and clearly.

'Although we did have papers for the child Lucy Clyde, we did not have the child. She definitely did not come with that party. There must have been an error. When we realised this we sent the papers on.'

'She is not here?' Kezzie asked dully.

'If it will make you more easy I will take you to meet

all of the children. None of them are at all close in age to your sister.'

Kezzie nodded. She must think. She must not panic. She had to think.

'It is too late for you to travel anywhere now,' he said. 'You are welcome to spend the night here, and then in the morning you can decide what to do.'

Kezzie gripped her bag tightly. She had already decided. There was only one thing she could do. Return to Montreal and start again.

22. On the train

By the time Kezzie returned to Montreal the Fitzwilliams had left for America. She went straight to the Receiving Home.

The officer in charge was sympathetic but regretful.

'This is just a clearing home,' he said. 'Sometimes they don't even come through here. They go directly to a home.' He checked the ledgers and found the record relating to Lucy Clyde. 'It was a mistake,' he said. 'The children from Liverpool and Scotland were regrouped to make a more even balance, and her papers were sent to Carrville in error. She must have gone with the other party, to a home in Dalton in British Columbia.'

Kezzie went back to Immigration. Yes, children had come through. A week or so ago. They had been in two groups, one going south, to Niagara, the other west, all the way to British Columbia.

Had Lucy definitely been with the other group, or was she somewhere else altogether? The confusion with the papers had upset Kezzie deeply. How could she be sure where her sister was? Was she even in search of the right person? Surely someone would recall seeing a child as pretty as Lucy?

It was a very distraught Kezzie who went through the Immigration sheds trying to find someone who could help her. Did anyone remember a little girl? Blonde, age about seven, blue eyes. She showed them the cracked and blurred photograph, taken at the seaside many months ago. The happy face smiling from behind the sandcastle didn't seem to be connected to her little sister at all. She couldn't even tell them what Lucy was wearing now.

Eventually she came across a tall bearded man with a faint Scottish burr in his voice. A little girl? He checked the files. There *was* a Lucy Clyde listed. Did he remember anything about her – anything at all? He thought carefully. There was one child he recalled, smaller than the rest, very pretty but poorly, clutching a rag doll. Kezzie's heart jumped. Lucy's doll! The one she had made her for her Christmas present. It had been missing from the caravan! He checked the records again. It must be her. The next older child was ten. Which way? Which way? Dalton, he was almost sure, B.C.

'You take the Canadian Pacific Railway. It goes all the way,' he said proudly, 'from sea to sea.'

Kezzie turned away. 'Poorly.' He had said Lucy was poorly. She had a great unease in her mind. Lucy was ill.

At the exit there was a huge map of Canada pinned to the wall, and as Kezzie stared at it she felt quite faint. British Columbia was hundreds and hundreds of miles away. She traced the line of the railway, she could barely make out Dalton. It was on the other side of the Rocky Mountains! A wave of dizziness swept over her.

'You all right, ma'am?'

:

She shook her head, trying to clear it.

Someone took her firmly by the elbow and led her away from the crowds to sit on one of the wooden benches which ran along the wall. A glass of water was put in her hand. Her fingers shook as she drank. She looked up. It was the tall immigration official.

'Thank you,' she said. 'I'm quite all right now.'

She made to stand up. He pushed her gently back down.

'With respect, ma'am, no you ain't,' he said. 'You're going to have to take it easy for a little while.'

'I cannot wait,' Kezzie said wildly. 'I have lost too much time already. You said yourself my sister was unwell. I must press on and find her. She may be in great danger.'

He consulted his pocket watch. 'The train for B.C. doesn't leave for some hours yet. Why don't we book you a ticket, then go and have something to eat? My guess is that you haven't breakfasted at all today.'

Kezzie hesitated. It was true. She couldn't remember when she had last eaten.

'I thought as much,' he smiled at her easily. 'Now

you ain't going to do your sister or yourself much good
if you collapse on the street and end up in hospital.'

Kezzie followed his broad figure as he shouldered
his way through the throngs of people. He organised
her ticket and baggage and then led the way to a small
restaurant close to Windsor railway station. It was
comforting to have someone take command, and as she
started to eat she found herself telling Alexander
Dalgleish all about her life.

'You are an amazing girl, Kezzie Munro,' he said. 'To
come all this way on your own.'

'But your country is so vast,' said Kezzie wearily. 'I
have already travelled hundreds of miles and I feel I am
as far away as ever from her. And,' she pointed out of
the window, 'there are so many people. I have never
seen so many people in my life. I could search for ever
and not find her.' She felt her eyes fill up with tears.

Impulsively he reached forward and gripped her
hand.

'I'm sure you'll find her,' he said. 'I have dealt with
the people involved in the juvenile immigration
scheme. Dr Barnardo's, Sheltering Homes and various

church organisations have brought many children to a better life in Canada. It has been going on for a long time and they are very well organised. The foster homes are carefully selected and they have an efficient after-care system of inspection. I'm sure Lucy is being well looked after.'

Later Alexander Dalgleish watched Kezzie make her way towards the train. Her long dark curls and elegant clothes made her stand out in the crowds. He sincerely hoped they would meet again. She was a fine-looking girl, with the type of spirit a developing country needed, and so concerned for her sister. He had not liked to tell her too much about the state of the child or the cuff on the side of the head which he had witnessed her receiving.

Although her nerves were fraught with worry, being on the train, as with being on the boat meant that Kezzie had time to sit and observe. In an attempt to distract her thoughts she leafed through the collection of newspapers and magazines in the restaurant car. Ontario's crop harvest was up on 1937's despite extensive damage by army worms. There were pictures of farmers taking in their harvest. They would be doing that at home, thought Kezzie, in the fields around her village.

Most of the rest was news of bombings and killing. In Germany Jews had been ordered to carry special identity cards. The British government had commissioned a thousand new Spitfire fighters. As more and more outrageous acts of hatred and aggression occurred, the whole world seemed to be racing towards war. Then an item in *The Globe and Mail* for Saturday, 6 August caught her eye. 'QUEEN'S READY' ran the headline. She smiled as she read the article. So her grandad's 'royal connection' was about to be launched from John Brown's yard on the Clyde. She felt better at once. It had given her a brief link with home which cheered her and she knew that all her friends and family would be thinking of her. She was still on edge at every stop but it eased her mind to know that at least she was making progress. Dalton was the end of Lucy's travels, surely she would catch her there?

Canada was beautiful, Kezzie had to acknowledge

the fact. She gazed from her window as the train took her across the face of the continent.

It was autumn, the Canadians called it the Fall. The country was coloured in crimson and gold. They passed Lake Superior at Heron Bay. On the Prairies the flat farmlands stretched to the horizon, with a farmhouse and little lakes dotted here and there. The train stopped at small towns with their tall grain elevators. Kezzie became accustomed to the bell sounding and the cheery call of the railwaymen. She consulted her map. The names intrigued her; Medicine Hat, Swift Current, Moose Jaw. Eating up the miles the train travelled across the country. She sometimes went to the observation car. She preferred to be there at night, or the early morning, with only the sound of the engine pulling and the wheels rattling for company. She would pray as she watched the sun rise on another day, but her prayers had no words, only a thought, a deep intent.

'Let Lucy be safe. Let Lucy be safe,' she whispered in time with the rhythm of the train.

23. Jane Smith

Lucy felt far from safe. The motion of the train for days had been only marginally better than that of the ship. When she had looked out of the window it seemed to her like another sea, a great expanse of grass and grain with waves which never stopped in the wind. She sat slumped, stupefied in her seat.

On arrival at the home their escort discovered that some of the children's papers were missing.

'Must have gone with the other group,' she fumed. 'I don't know, the organisation gets worse. I'm due to go back to Montreal. I'll have to leave you to sort something out.'

:

The matron shrugged. It was not the first time she would have to assign new names and ages to unknown children. She was understaffed and the Canadian government now frowned on child immigration. She would try to place these ones as quickly as possible. With the homes being run down perhaps she would be able to retire soon. Each batch of children appeared to her to have more problems and be more undisciplined than the last.

The rougher ones gave her the greatest headache. One boy called Jack had been sent back three times by the people she had put him with. A dark swarthy little creature, who constantly stole anything and everything left unattended, she despaired of ever placing him. He had obviously been badly abused at some time and trusted no one.

She had given the new group a quick assessment on arrival. The older boys were very rude, but seemed quite strong. Perhaps some of the logging camps would take on a few lads. It was a good job. Hard work, but fairly paid and out in the open air. These children were so pale and undernourished. She thought they must come from some of the worst slums in Europe. She had heard that Glasgow had a bad record of child mortality. Houses built too close together blocking the sun, and lack of milk and undernourishment meant that many children suffered from rickets. Well, at least here they had a chance to thrive in the clear air.

The children were playing outside. She glanced out of the window. The child with the doll who shrank in the corner of the yard, staring around her vacantly, was going to be difficult to get rid of. Though she recalled an outback couple who had been looking for a girl to train as a servant. They certainly weren't the type you would want one of your own to go to, but an idiot child like that would have to take what she could get. She'd contact them tomorrow.

Lucy stood as far away from everyone as she could possibly get. Only one other child, a boy of about nine, did not join in with the rest either. He was sallow and skinny, with black hair and furtive eyes. He played with a ball at the edge of the yard, talking all the while to himself.

'Atsit,' Jack would say, as he bounced the ball against the wall. 'Gerronyer.'

If anyone came near him or tried to take his ball he would snarl in a most ferocious manner. Jack had been in the home the longest and had established certain territorial rights.

'Goal!' he cried as the ball soared up and over the fence.

Lucy watched him vaguely as he climbed over to retrieve it. On the way back he slipped and crashed heavily to the ground. The ball fell from his grasp and bounced towards her. Instinctively she put up her hands and caught it. She waited but he did not get up. She stood still, not sure what to do, and then walked slowly towards him. He rolled over, his face screwed up in pain. There was a deep gash on his leg. She looked round for help.

'Don't tell. Don't tell,' he said quickly. 'I'll sort it myself.' He took a grubby hanky from his pocket and spat on it. 'I'll catch it for climbing the fence if they find out. Then I'll get locked in the cupboard.' He mopped up the blood. 'Don't like bein' in the cupboard, 's dark an' all. You won't tell, will ye?'

:

Lucy shook her head.

At dinner that night Lucy was by chance beside him. He ate his food noisily and greedily. She picked up her spoon slowly, meanwhile gazing about her, trying to make sense of where she was. She looked down at her plate. She didn't recognise this kind of food. It wasn't like anything Kezzie had given her to eat. A lump of brown meat lay half submerged in gravy. She looked around her hopelessly. Grandad always cut up her meat for her.

There was a piece of bread beside her plate. She reached to pick it up and as she did so the boy from the ship stretched across the table and grabbed it from her.

'Ha! Ha!' he crowed.

As he went to put it into his mouth, Jack with a quick movement punched him on the face, took the bread back and gave it to Lucy.

'Quick,' he said, 'eat it fast.'

Lucy gobbled her bread.

The other boy got up and came round the table towards Jack. He was much bigger and heavier. Jack did not move until the boy was beside him. Then he swung round and kicked him viciously with his hobnailed tackety boots, and leaping to his feet shouted, 'Matron, that boy's out of his seat!'

The matron hurried over. She regarded Jack suspiciously. He continued eating his dinner with an air of innocence. The other boy gave him a look of hatred.

Jack grinned at Lucy.

'Has yer doll got a name?' he asked nodding to Lucy's constant companion.

Lucy looked at her doll sadly. She was stained and smelly. Her clothes were torn. She had lost one eye and her hair was falling out.

'Kissy,' she whispered.

Just before bedtime Jack was ambushed in the washrooms. Lucy could only stare mutely as Matron dragged him out of the middle of the fight. The boy from the ship had a bloody nose and there was a bruise rising on her protector's eye.

'He started it, didn't he?' the bigger boy asked the rest menacingly. They nodded.

'It's the punishment room for you, my lad,' said the

matron dragging him down the corridor, 'and you can stay in there for two days this time.' Lucy watched from a distance.

As Kezzie's train entered the high passes of the Rocky Mountains the matron in the home in Dalton made arrangements for Lucy's adoption.

'Jane Smith is the child's name,' she told the couple before her. 'Though you can change it if you will.' She looked at them. They were mean and shabby but the child was lucky to get even that. She rang her bell. 'I'll get someone to bring her down.'

When she was sent for Lucy came from the top of the house where she had been scrubbing the floors. She passed the cupboard at the bottom of the stairs in which Jack was locked. She thought of him in the dark, all alone for such a long time. She remembered herself in the coffin ship with only her dolly beside her. There was a little snib on the door. She gazed at it, a small figure in black button boots and a white pinafore covering her brown orphan's dress. She looked up and down the corridor and then carefully opened the door. Jack was crouched in the corner with his hands over his head. His face was streaked and blotched. Without a word Lucy handed him her doll and then went away.

24. The rag doll

Kezzie folded down her couchette bed for the last time. Tomorrow she would be in Dalton, she had travelled over two thousand miles in the last few days. She felt a great peace inside, brought about by the fact that she knew she was close to the end of her travels but also by this great country itself.

Each person she had spoken to in Canada was so very proud of their nation, from Janine and Alexander Dalgleish to her fellow travellers on the train.

'Sure we have still got those tin-and-tarpaper shanty towns on the outskirts of the big cities,' a construction worker she had met in the dining-car had told her, 'but our fish canning and tannery works are expanding. This year the Bank of Canada has been fully nationalised. They'll control the credit rates so we're going to make progress out of the Great Depression.'

The train conductor had talked of the opening up of the country. A trans-Canada Air Line had recently been established, and now with the Canadian Broadcasting Corporation being publicly owned it beamed a great variety of programmes and news right into the remotest areas. He had been with the railways all his life and had watched as the ranchers followed each new track laid. Central Canada was now a vast chessboard of growing crops, warmed in spring by the strong gusty wind known as the snow eater, which blew down from the Rockies, and which the Indians called the Chinook.

He told her to look out for Calgary, its Gaelic name meaning preserved pasture at the harbour.

It was still very much a frontier town and had been originally a fort for the North West Mounted Police. They had had to control the wild wolf hunters from

Montana, and the American whisky traders who created unrest among the native tribes, the Blackfoot, Salish and Sarcee. Soon after that she would see the most beautiful part of Canada as the train would swing in a great loop north and enter the eastern foothills of the Rocky Mountains.

The territories through which the train had passed seemed to show nature's every part. Vermilion foliage, golden plains stretching out to the limits of the earth, rivers, forests, lakes and the jagged peaks of the Canadian Rocky Mountains. The sky was a blue canopy without horizons above her when she wandered down the track to stretch her legs at the various stops. At night the air was clear and cold and the stars seemed bright and close.

The train had reached Banff, climbed past Lake Louise to the highest point at the Great Divide of the Atlantic and Pacific watersheds. The conductor had pointed out to her the stream, parted, one to flow east to the Hudson Bay, one to flow west to the Pacific. Descending from the steep Kicking Horse Pass via the spiral tunnels, over many mountain ravines and then

:

back up through the Selkirks to the Connaught Tunnel under Mount Macdonald. Kezzie had gazed back at the carriages snaking behind the engines across the vast gorge at Stoney Creek Bridge. What engineering skills and fortitude it had taken to conquer these mountains!

She hardly slept at all that night and was dressed and fully packed as the train drew in to Dalton early the next morning. It was a strange thing, thought Kezzie, as she made her enquiries firstly at the station office and then the town hall, how one's clothes mattered. Lady Fitzwilliam had bought her the most expensive costume she could find, with matching shoes, gloves, hat and handbag. And it seemed to Kezzie that people *were* more respectful and attentive to her. It was unfair, she thought.

She arrived at the Distribution Home, a grey forbidding house with iron railings all around. Kezzie gazed up at the windows. Was Lucy behind one of those faded net curtains?

'You've come all the way from Scotland?' the matron said in disbelief. 'Well, I'm sorry to disappoint you but I can't give just anybody access to my records or to the children in my care.'

Kezzie nodded calmly and handed her the letter from Lady Fitzwilliam.

'You know this person?' The matron hesitated.

Kezzie looked her straight in the face. 'A relative, actually,' she lied.

The matron flicked through her books slowly.

'No one of that name has been here at all,' she said finally.

'There must be some mistake,' said Kezzie, now quite frightened. 'The Immigration in Montreal told me, and Lady Fitzwilliam,' she added quickly, 'that she had come here.'

The matron hesitated.

'Papers sometimes go astray,' she said. 'The records are not always . . . quite accurate. Names and personal details may change. There have been two or three children of about that age. One is still here.' She rang her bell.

Kezzie examined the forlorn child with the red pigtails who stood in front of her.

'That is not Lucy,' she said.

'There was one other child of about that age who passed through my hands recently,' said the matron, 'but she had been given the name Jane.'

'Can you describe her?' asked Kezzie.

The matron thought for a minute. 'She was quite small . . .'

'Blue eyes?' Kezzie asked anxiously.

'I think so . . . Yes.'

'Her hair,' continued Kezzie excitedly, 'little blonde curls all over her head. She is a beautiful child.'

The matron sighed. The child she was thinking about had not been beautiful at all.

'I don't think so,' she said. 'In fact I'm sure this child's hair was brown, it was certainly quite lank, and she was not attractive at all.' She paused for a second. 'Was there anything wrong with your sister?'

'Pardon?' said Kezzie.

The matron cleared her throat.

'It's just that this child was . . . well, not quite right.'

'What do you mean?'

'The child was mentally retarded, and had no speech.'

'No!' cried Kezzie.

:

'Well, that's it then.' The matron closed her book with finality.

Kezzie stood up from the chair stiffly. Her body and brain was numb. To come so far . . .

'Would you like some tea?' the matron asked more kindly.

Kezzie shook her head. She had to find somewhere quiet. She had to sit and think. What would she write to Grandad and Bella after her first hopeful telegram? Had they made a mistake in Montreal? Was Lucy in Carrville? Was she even in Canada?

She waited in the hallway while the maid brought her coat and suitcase from the back. Kezzie looked round at the scrubbed lino floors and the polished wooden banisters. Very clean, too clean for children to play in. Not a happy place for someone like Lucy. Was she in another similar place on the other side of Canada? Kezzie had fought through their months of starvation to save Lucy from a fate such as this. A spartan orphanage, a sham of a 'home'. She had failed her. Had she made a bad mistake? Was Lucy still in Scotland? Where was her sister?

The maid helped her on with her coat. Kezzie's arms were leaden. She could scarcely think. As she picked up her suitcase she heard a snuffling noise from the small cupboard under the stairwell.

Kezzie looked at the maid questioningly. The maid dropped her eyes. Kezzie glanced towards the front door where the matron was waiting to see her out.

There it was again, a strange whimpering sound. Kezzie reached forward and opened the cupboard door.

There was a small boy crouched in the corner. He covered his face with his hands as the light shone on him.

'There is a boy in this cupboard,' said Kezzie.

The matron hurried forward, tutting.

'Yes, yes. That is the punishment cupboard. And that is a particularly bad boy. He is often in there.'

Kezzie was horrified. 'You lock children in a cupboard because they are naughty?'

'He is more than naughty. He is bad. Don't criticise what you don't have to deal with.'

Kezzie stepped back reluctantly. It was none of her

business, but the boy seemed so frightened and pathetic. As she turned away he reached out his hand towards the light, and the thing he was holding fell to the floor.

Kezzie picked it up and leaned forward to give it to him. And then she stopped . . . She looked more closely at the object in her hand. A raggedy doll with torn dirty clothes . . . and one blue button eye which gazed at her unblinking.

'Where did you get this?' she asked the boy hoarsely.

He shrank from her into the furthest corner of the cupboard. Kezzie knelt down and reaching in tucked the doll firmly back into his arms.

'I'm not going to keep it,' she said quietly. 'It's yours.'

She waited for a moment.

'I knew a little girl who had a doll just like yours,' she said softly. 'Perhaps you met her?'

He only stared back at her.

'I know that she would have liked you for a friend,' Kezzie went on easily. 'And she would have given her doll to someone to watch for her, or . . .' Kezzie thought desperately. 'Or keep them company in a dark place.'

Something in his eyes changed.

'I just wondered,' Kezzie said carefully, 'does this doll have a name?'

There was a long silence. Then the answer came softly.

'Her name's Kissy.'

25. The farmstead

'That's the place you're lookin' for.'

Kezzie surveyed the farmstead to which the hired waggon driver from Dalton was pointing with his buggy whip. It was a very run-down-looking homestead, she thought. The paint on the wooden slats, which made up the walls, was bleached and flaking. The curtains in the windows were torn and dirty. There was no garden to speak of, just weeds and broken bits of crockery and tools lying about the yard.

'You are sure this is the place?'

'Yup. That's the Tchekov's section. Beats me why

someone like you is visiting with folks like them.' He spat a long squirt of tobacco juice on to the side of the road. 'Ain't none o' my business though.'

Kezzie climbed down from the waggon.

'Will you wait here for me please? I won't be long.'

She picked her way carefully towards the front door. There was a faint trace of smoke coming from the chimney, but apart from that she could see no sign of life. Kezzie rapped on the door. Nothing happened. She knocked louder, and glanced back at the waggon driver. He was staring at the horizon. She rattled the catch and the door fell open. Kezzie's first reaction was to turn and leave such was the scene of squalor which met her eyes. The room was filthy, the floor unswept for many months, the chair covers and linen unwashed. Food, clothing, pots and pans lay about everywhere. She stepped inside.

'Here what do you think you're doing?'

There was a woman stirring a pot on the fire in the corner.

'I'm sorry,' said Kezzie. 'I knocked on the door. No one answered so I came in . . .' she trailed off and looked around her. Could Lucy possibly be in a place like this?

The woman's eyes narrowed as she looked at Kezzie.

'What do you want here?' She advanced on Kezzie with the ladle still in her hand. 'What call has the likes of you got to come around here?'

Kezzie stood her ground.

'I've come from the home in Dalton,' she said. Well, it wasn't quite a lie. 'I've come to see the little girl you took.'

The woman relaxed her grip on the ladle.

'The home child,' she said. 'That was a bad deal we got there, not much work in her, always poorly, needin' feed.' She tapped her forehead. 'Ain't able to talk, not right in the head neither.'

'Where is she?' asked Kezzie as calmly as she could. Her heart was pounding.

'Out in the lean-to.' The woman stared at Kezzie. 'What do you want to see her for? What business is it of yours?'

Kezzie smoothed her gloves into her fingers and held her head up and stared straight back at the woman.

'I told you,' she said firmly. 'I am from the home. Now take me to her at once.'

The woman led the way through the yard to a lean-to at the back of the house. Here, scraggy chickens pecked in the dirt and an old cat with matted fur slunk away under the house.

The woman pushed the door of the shed open.

'She ain't been well the last few days,' she whined. 'I've been having to nurse her. That was soup I was making her, extra work for me on top of everything else I have to do.'

Kezzie barely heard her. She had stepped past her into the darkness. By the light from the door she could see a straw mattress on which a small figure lay huddled, half-sitting against the wall. The air was foetid, it was a place one would not have kept animals in. A stench of urine and vomit made Kezzie gag. She went forward slowly and looked at the child in the bed. She was smaller and thinner than Lucy had been. Her hair was coarse and tufted and moving with lice. Her face was sallow and sunken, her skin was lacerated and covered with scabs. But worse, much worse, were the child's eyes. They stared blankly out at nothing. The woman was right. This child was indeed an idiot.

Kezzie felt anger. Anger at the woman who had treated a child so badly, and anger at the authorities which had allowed a child to be placed with people such as these. She would go straight back to Dalton, but not to the home. She would go to the police and report this. She turned towards the door. And then the fact of the matter hit her.

If this child was not her sister, then where in the wide world was Lucy? She had followed the trail very carefully and had not found her. Where could she be? Not in Scotland, not in Canada. Where? There was nowhere else left for Kezzie to search. Lucy was lost to her for ever.

Kezzie paused with her hand on the door. A feeling of the greatest despair came over her. The woman was watching her. Kezzie put her forehead against her hand and bowed her head in defeat.

There was a silence in the room. Nothing. Kezzie felt a breath against her cheek. She sensed something . . . an echo. She raised her head. The woman had not moved. She glanced in the corner of the shed. Neither had the child. Then what? Kezzie looked at the woman.

'Did the child say something?' she asked her.

'I told you,' said the woman. 'She be dumb . . .'

Kezzie held up her hand to silence her and walked towards the bed.

'Did you speak, little girl?'

The child gazed at her vacantly.

Kezzie knelt down beside the child's bed. She took one thin hand in both hers.

'Little girl,' she said gently. 'Did you say something?'

There was a terrible empty silence in the room. Kezzie felt as though the world had stopped turning. She moved her head slightly to try to catch the child's gaze. Was there something there? Was her imagination playing tricks? A gleam of light in the eyes. Was it a reflection of something? Kezzie felt at her throat for her little silver locket. She held it up before the child's eyes.

'See,' she said.

Nothing.

Kezzie sat back on her heels. She closed her eyes.

She could feel the warm tears beginning to trickle through her lids.

'Oh, Lucy, where are you?' she whispered.

Then she heard, no more than a breath on the air, a sigh. One word.

'Kezzie.'

26. Papers

Kezzie opened her eyes very slowly. The child was staring at her fixedly. Kezzie reached out her arm and the child seemed to shrink away from her. Kezzie longed to hold her sister and hug her, and cry and shout with joy, but something told her that it would be the wrong thing to do.

'Lucy, Lucy,' she said softly. 'I've come for you. I've come to take you home.' And very gently she stroked her sister's cheek with the back of her hand.

Lucy looked around her with wide frightened eyes. She struggled to speak again.

'Home?' she said. She closed her eyes.

Kezzie stood up and brushed her skirt down.

'I want to take this child away now,' she said to the woman.

'You can't,' the woman said. 'You need papers, or something.' She had a sly look on her face.

Kezzie thought quickly.

'I have them,' she said firmly. 'In my bag.'

By the Lord God, she decided, I am taking Lucy away from here if I have to knock this person down.

'Show me,' said the woman.

Kezzie looked at Lucy lying on the mattress. Her eyes were half-closed. She appeared to have lost consciousness.

'We will discuss it in the house,' said Kezzie and walked out of the lean-to.

They went round the side of the shack.

'I'm going to speak to the driver for one minute,' said Kezzie. She went to the buggy. 'I have some business to discuss with that woman,' she said to the driver. 'While I am doing that I want you to take the travelling rug, go to the lean-to at the back and wrap up the child who is there and put her in the buggy.'

The driver looked at her for a long minute.

'It is quite legal,' said Kezzie, 'she is my sister.'

The driver hesitated.

'I'll double your fare,' said Kezzie desperately. Then she said, 'She is my sister. She was put up for adoption by mistake. I have come from Scotland to find her.'

'All right,' he said.

Kezzie went back to the house.

'Show me your papers,' said the woman.

Kezzie took out the letter written by Lady Fitzwilliam. The woman glanced at it, and something in the way she did caught Kezzie's attention.

'I don't know,' said the woman, 'doesn't seem right to me.'

Kezzie saw her ship's boarding pass lying at the bottom of her bag. She placed it in front of the woman.

'This is the official form from the home which we both sign, and you may keep it as proof that you handed the child over to me.'

Kezzie held her breath. The woman studied it for a second or two.

'That's official then?' she asked.

Kezzie let her breath out slowly. She had guessed correctly. The woman could not read. She took the fountain pen which William had given her and signed the boarding pass with a flourish.

'You sign the bottom or make your mark,' she said. Then with a flash of inspiration, she added, 'And of course you are due payment. I am authorised to give you twenty dollars.'

Kezzie counted the money out on to the table. Any reservations which the woman might have had vanished completely. She picked up the money quickly.

Kezzie stood up.

'My driver has taken the little girl out to the buggy. I will take my leave of you.'

It required all of Kezzie's willpower not to run down the path. She climbed in the back where the driver had laid Lucy and stroked her hair and talked to her all the way back to town.

'Dearest child, beautiful child,' Kezzie murmured, stroking Lucy's hair.

'Which room you in?' asked the driver as they stopped outside the hotel.

Kezzie told him and he carried Lucy straight up.

'I'd say that child needs a doctor,' he said as he went towards the door.

'I intend to get her one right away,' said Kezzie. She opened her purse. 'I have another three dollars to give you.'

He shook his head. He looked at Kezzie.

'You come all the way from Scotland to get her?'

Kezzie nodded.

'Ain't no more'n a child yourself,' he said and went out closing the door behind him.

Kezzie bathed Lucy gently with a cloth as she waited for the doctor's arrival. At first she had thought to get on the first train and put as much distance between herself and this town as she could, but Lucy's condition seemed to worsen. Her breathing was shallow and she could never have travelled in the condition she was in.

There was a rap on the door.

'Dr McMath. There is a sick child here?' The man was about sixty with silver hair and glasses.

'My sister,' said Kezzie.

The doctor drew his breath in sharply as he examined Lucy. He gave Kezzie a severe look.

'What exactly is going on here?'

'She was put in an orphanage in Scotland by mistake when I was involved in an accident. They sent her to Canada, and some terrible people adopted her, and I got her back today.' Kezzie could hear her own voice begin to shake. 'I . . . I . . . is she very sick?'

'She will need to go to hospital,' said Dr McMath. 'There is more than physical sickness here. What you tell me explains it a little. She is deeply traumatised, shock, you know.'

He took off his glasses and put them in his top pocket.

'No hospital,' said Kezzie at once. 'I will nurse her here. She is not going to a hospital. She is not going anywhere away from me.'

'Young lady . . .' began the doctor. He was interrupted by a loud knocking on the door.

Before either of them could move the door was opened abruptly and a man in blue heavily soiled work overalls stood there.

'You,' he shouted pointing at Kezzie. 'You were at my place today and took my girl. Well, I've come to take her back. This ain't legal.'

And to Kezzie's horror she saw that he was holding in his hand her ship's boarding pass.

27. The doctor's house

Kezzie stepped between the man and the bed where her sister lay. She felt herself go rigid with fright. She looked down at Lucy lying so still, barely making any indent on the bed. Kezzie felt as though Lucy was almost unreal, a frail little spirit held into its body only by her, Kezzie's will ... and now, she felt herself faltering.

Dr McMath's voice when he spoke surprised her. It was polite and gentle, very gentle.

'What's the matter, John?' He went towards the farmer. 'Something wrong?'

'I got that girl, fair and square from the home. You know the trouble we've had, we've got no help on our place. Now, she ain't been much use, but she's ours. I don't know if this is legal.' He waved the boarding pass again in the doctor's face.

Dr McMath took Kezzie's boarding pass from John Tchekov's hand. He held it carefully.

'What is this?' he asked.

Kezzie held her breath.

'It's her authority, she says.' The farmer pointed at Kezzie. 'She come and took the child and this gave her leave to do it, she says.'

The doctor studied the card.

'I . . .' he started.

'Fifteen dollars ain't enough,' said the farmer.

'Fifteen dollars?' said Dr McMath.

'Twenty,' said Kezzie immediately. 'I paid twenty.'

'Twenty?' asked the farmer. 'She only said fifteen.'

'Twenty,' said Kezzie firmly. 'That's what the home told me,' she added quickly.

'The home told you?' Dr McMath raised an eyebrow.

'Twenty?' said the farmer once again. 'She said fifteen.'

'I paid your wife twenty dollars,' said Kezzie, thinking to herself, you are not going past me.

Dr McMath groped in his pockets for a minute or two.

'I don't seem to have my glasses,' he said slowly. He held up the pass to the light and squinted at it. 'It's certainly an official document of some sort, John,' he said. 'What I'll do is this. I'll hold on to it just now and investigate this properly for you. In the meantime, you couldn't take this child back with you anyroad. She is quite ill. I will have to take charge of her.' With that the doctor put the boarding pass in his pocket and led the farmer to the door.

'She was poorly when she came to us,' said the farmer. 'It's not our fault.'

'I'm sure it's not,' said the doctor soothingly. 'You never ill-treated a living thing in your life, John.' He saw the farmer out. 'I'll call by later in the week and see you.'

Dr McMath came back into the room. He took his

glasses from his pocket and studied Kezzie's boarding pass carefully. Then he said, 'Now, young lady, I'd like you to tell me exactly how you and your sister got here.'

Twenty minutes later Kezzie and Lucy, wrapped in a travelling rug and several blankets, were on their way in the doctor's car to his house in the nearby village of Waterfoot.

His wife, Sarah, a plump grey-haired woman came to meet them. Kezzie liked her at once. She asked no questions but only took Lucy from her sister's arms, carried her upstairs and put her to bed. Dr McMath followed. He gave Lucy some clear medicine and then they all went downstairs to the kitchen.

'I don't know how people can behave like that to a child,' said Kezzie pacing up and down.

'Ignorance,' sighed the doctor. 'True ignorance, and of course the Depression.'

'That's no excuse,' fumed Kezzie. 'The place was not clean. We were as poor but we did not let ourselves get into such a state.'

The doctor's wife said nothing as she set out a meal of potatoes and pie.

The doctor regarded Kezzie gravely.

'Perhaps you do not appreciate exactly what it is like to live through hard times. Farming in Canada has suffered from real drought. Plagues of grasshoppers and a lessening demand for wheat. At one stage the Prairies were in total financial collapse. The amount of small farms lost to mortgage companies was colossal. All over Canada men were riding the rails. Travelling on the roofs of the freight trains in freezing cold looking for jobs that did not exist.'

Kezzie was silent. She remembered the bothy they had stayed in, and how she had felt the start of their slow slide into misery. Only having a sliver of soap and no hot water. Being utterly tired, day after day. The amount of energy needed to dress and change oneself, when lack of food and lack of purpose was ever present. What would have happened to them had their fortunes not changed? She recalled the people in some of the streets in Glasgow, the hopeless and helpless slouch of the men on the street corners.

'Britain is rearming,' continued Dr McMath, 'and whatever you may think of that, it does provide

:

employment.' He paused. 'Besides which . . .' He got up and went to look out of the window. 'I helped John Tchekov bury eight children in the field behind his farm, not one of them lived more than a year. I reckon his wife was looking for something to love and just couldn't cope when it went wrong on her.'

Kezzie put her head in her hands. She felt ashamed, instead of triumphant at having found Lucy. She was overcome with weariness and worry.

Mrs McMath brought a cot bed for Kezzie and placed it beside the bed in which Lucy lay. Kezzie drifted into a troubled sleep gazing at her sister and woke in the morning still tired. Lucy was no better.

Kezzie wrote to Grandad via Bella telling him where they were but not giving much detail of what had happened. She said that Lucy was improving. She could not bear to write the truth.

Another day passed the same way. Dr McMath was worried. Kezzie could see that. He had dosed Lucy regularly and at least her breathing seemed easier. Kezzie, who scarcely left Lucy's side, mentioned this to him.

He frowned. 'It's not her bodily health which concerns me the most,' he said. 'It is the child's spirit. She has put a barrier between herself and reality because life became too painful for her. We have to work at removing it. If we can,' he added.

It was true, thought Kezzie. Even though Lucy spoke now, it was only a 'yes' or a 'no' and that very reluctantly. Mostly she lay propped up in bed in a half-dream. Kezzie could have wept when she thought of the little girl who had screamed with delight on the roller coaster or gone with her jam jar to search for tadpoles in the burn.

'I am going in to Dalton,' the doctor told her a few days later. 'I'm going to speak to a few people and see if I can do something about having that rescue home closed. I thought most of these places had gone, apart from the farm school on Vancouver Island. They're obviously not screening applicants properly and I doubt if they are sending out inspectors to check on the children they have placed.'

28. Jack

Later that same evening the telephone rang. Kezzie heard Sarah McMath call her from the hall.

'It's the doctor. He wants to speak to you.'

Kezzie took the handpiece from her. The doctor was calling from Dalton. The home was being closed. All the children were placed and accounted for. Except one. Did Kezzie remember seeing a boy called Jack?

'It seems as though the child has run away,' said Dr McMath. 'They're very worried, what with winter coming on.'

Kezzie tried to remember. She couldn't really recall

any of the children's names at the home. The only little boy she remembered distinctly was the boy in the cupboard ... and he was locked in ... She suddenly realised that he would be exactly the type of child who would run away.

'Can you describe him?' she asked.

It was Jack, of course. Kezzie spoke to the matron who sounded dreadfully worried. Kezzie felt sorry for her. The woman was trying to justify her treatment of the boy.

'I had to lock him up,' she said. 'He was violent towards other children. What could I do?'

What else, indeed? thought Kezzie as she replaced the telephone on its stand. Perhaps spoken to him, cuddled him? Maybe he was rough and aggressive. All Kezzie had seen in the cupboard was a very scared and lonely small boy.

She went slowly into the front parlour where Mrs McMath was sewing.

'The doctor is going to stay on a little while in Dalton to see if they turn up any trace of the boy,' she said. The lamp was on in the room. Kezzie went to draw the curtains. She looked out of the window. It was dark and cold with a heavy sky threatening rain. Was Jack outside in this weather, with little protection in his thin orphanage clothes?

Sarah McMath got up and came and stood behind her. She put her arms round Kezzie.

'He'll be all right,' she said. 'If anyone can find him, my Andrew will.'

Three days passed before Dr McMath returned home.

Kezzie was sitting at the side of Lucy's bed reading to her. She was not sure if her sister was listening as Lucy's eyes were almost closed. She hesitated as she turned the page. Then she heard voices outside the bedroom door.

'Go on in,' she heard Dr McMath say.

The door opened and a scruffy boy entered cautiously. Kessie saw her sister's eyes open, and then widen in surprise.

Jack advanced into the room in a cocky manner.

'So this is where ye went,' he said looking around, 'not bad for some, eh?' He went about the room picking things up and examining them. He went to the window and looked out at the yard and the garden. 'Not bad, not bad,' he said. Then he sat down on the end of Lucy's bed. 'Here! This is real soft. Bet ye wish ye were back in Dalton, an' I don't think.' He leaned forward. 'Look you,' he said, 'if they don't treat you right, tell *me*. I'll sort 'em out. I can fight anyone. That big one there,' he pointed at Kezzie, 'or even the old codger with the glasses.'

To Kezzie's amazement Lucy smiled.

'I got somethin' for ye.' Jack reached inside his pullover and brought out the rag doll. 'She's a bit mussed up,' he apologised, 'but that was on account of me having to hide her from the dragon lady.'

Lucy gave a piteous little cry and took the doll from him. The three of them watched her as she stroked its hair and cuddled it to her and mumbled nonsense words in its ear in a sing-song voice.

'I think,' said Dr McMath, 'that we may just have found the key to unlock this child's mind.'

They left Jack sitting beside Lucy's bed drinking milk and munching home-made cookies. He was full of himself, chattering away to her. He didn't take note of any strangeness in her manner and was so brimming over with life and mischief that she was forced to pay attention to him. He was starting to tell her of his adventures. Of how he had climbed down a forty-foot wall to run away and met up with hungry bears and wolves in the woods around Dalton.

Mrs McMath set out some food on the kitchen table.

'However did you find him?' she asked her husband.

'Well,' the doctor replied with a certain smugness, 'I reckoned with the whole of the Royal Mounties out lookin' for him they would cover all the obvious places, the logging camps and the railway stations. So there wasn't any use in me following them about. Then I sat down and thought to myself: "What would *I* do if I was that boy and I decided to run away?" After that it was easy.'

'Tell us,' said Kezzie, pouring out the coffee.

'I reckoned he would head this way, of course,' said Dr McMath. 'He's a smart boy. Most troublesome children like that are. They've a lot of energy that needs good direction, that's all. After Kezzie told me what she knew on the telephone, I just worked out that he would try to follow the only two people who had ever shown him any kindness.'

He took a long drink of his coffee.

Mrs McMath walked briskly round the table and took the cup from his hand.

'Andrew McMath. Kezzie and me, we have been worried sick these last days. If you don't leave off drinking that coffee and tell us the rest of this story at once, you will get absolutely no dinner this night.'

The doctor laughed.

'Well, I only drove very slowly up and down the road from Dalton to Waterfoot several times, stopping here and there to have a picnic, and making sure that the food was on plain view. It must have been the sight of those blueberry muffins you made, Sarah, because sure enough, on the second day a small figure appears as cheeky as you like and asks if I'd be passing through Waterfoot, because he might just do me the honour of accepting a lift from me.'

29. Christmas

The first trails of snow saw Lucy up and walking about. Jack was a tonic to everybody. To begin with he drove Dr and Mrs McMath to distraction. Nothing was safe from him. Ornaments fell from tables and broke as he passed, windows cracked of their own accord when he played football in the yard.

One day Kezzie was helping Mrs McMath put the winter quilts on the beds. They were in the small attic room where Jack slept, when on turning the mattress they discovered a vast quantity of food crushed under the bed. Most of it was rotten or had mould growing on it.

Mrs McMath sat down heavily in a small chair.

'Lord, Lord,' she said. 'What does that tell you, Kezzie?' she asked.

'That he is a thief,' said Kezzie reluctantly.

The older woman shook her head.

'It tells me that at some time he has starved.'

Jack came into the room at this moment and immediately turned for flight.

'Jack!' Mrs McMath called sternly.

He crept back, with such a look of fear on his face that Kezzie had to turn her head away.

'Come with me,' Mrs McMath commanded him. She led him downstairs through the kitchen to the pantry. 'Do you see this door?' she asked him. 'It is never locked. That means that anyone who lives here may go inside and eat as much as they please – whenever they choose. Do you understand me?'

He nodded warily.

'Eat as much as you want, Jack. Eat until your belly's sore and you cannot swallow another crumb.' She laughed and patted him on the head. 'And then go in and eat some more,' she said.

They went sleigh riding just before Christmas. Dressed Eskimo-style in hooded parkas they whizzed down the lanes and roads with the bells jingling. The runners hissed on the hard-packed snow and in the background the mountain ice caps shone diamond blue. They were on an expedition to the forest to cut down their own Christmas tree. Jack and Dr McMath spent some time studying various trees and discussing the merits of each, until eventually his wife called from the sleigh that the girls were getting cold, and if they didn't take the axe to a tree right this minute she was driving home without them. They selected a fine Douglas fir and brought it home.

The streets and buildings were decorated and brightly lit, and as they came back through the town their breaths frosted on the air with 'oohs' and 'aahs' as they saw the different coloured baubles and lights in the shop windows.

On Christmas Eve they exchanged small gifts. Kezzie had knitted the doctor a pair of fingerless mittens and embroidered a book mark for his wife. She had, against her better judgement, bought Jack a penknife. His face when he opened up the parcel made up for any doubts she may have had.

Lucy had crept on to Sarah McMath's knee and was opening her presents. Kezzie felt a tremendous pang of jealousy as she watched them. The little girl was looking up into the face of the older woman, who was stroking her hair and reading her the Christmas story from a book they had given her. She was aware of Dr McMath's hand on her shoulder.

'Are you not opening your present, Kezzie?' he asked gently.

Kezzie fumbled with the bulky parcel and pulled the wrapping away. It was a chess set. The pieces had been carved in soapstone by Eskimo craftsmen, the original Canadians the doctor had said.

'Perhaps with this set I might win a few games,' said the doctor.

Kezzie looked at him. They understood each other very well, she thought. He seemed to know when she was troubled or upset or homesick, and would suggest a walk or a game of chess to lift her mind.

After Christmas Kezzie counted her savings. Buying

herself and Lucy winter clothes had used up most of her money.

'I must look for work,' she announced at breakfast. 'You have been more than generous with us, but I cannot allow this to go on.'

The doctor and his wife exchanged glances.

'We thought you might say this one day,' said Sarah McMath eventually. 'We were going to make a proposition to you.' She glanced at her husband.

'I need help with my surgery, Kezzie. Sarah says she is getting too old and her eyesight is not as good as it was for dispensing. So, if you are agreeable to work with me, I could pay you a small wage.'

'Only if you deduct money for our keep,' said Kezzie firmly. Her heart was beating very fast. To work with a doctor and learn about medicine!

'And Jack,' said Mrs McMath. 'We must do something about him, also.'

They found Jack work at the local grocery store owned by Miss Hannah Chiltern, a lady who spoke to him severely but petted him in quite a ridiculous manner. He lodged in a room above the store and now considered himself an independent gentleman. He wore a long calico apron and would rush forward to serve them when Kezzie and Lucy did the shopping. Kezzie had to try not to laugh, but Lucy absolutely adored him. She took him very seriously and would insist on buying whatever Jack recommended, or what he said was a good buy that day. He was immensely proud of the bicycle which he used to deliver orders, and no matter what his destination always managed to ride past the doctor's house at least once a day.

Lucy spent more and more time with Mrs McMath in the kitchen, helping her bake or getting under her feet mainly, Kezzie thought. She was growing stronger as each day passed, fed on the good natural produce of the country, milk and eggs and the fruit stored for winter, pears and plums and apples.

Dr McMath had started to train Kezzie to help in the dispensary. She was now quite deft at using the little brass scales with their tiny weights and measured out the powders accurately. She was learning the names of drugs, complicated Latin terms and Greek symbols. She felt excited and thrilled at being surrounded by such vast quantities of knowledge. She could learn so much here.

One day Miss Chiltern came to see the doctor. She had Jack firmly by the collar. Kezzie felt her heart drop. What trouble had he been up to now?

'Do you know,' declared Miss Chiltern, 'that this here boy can't read or write?'

'Doesn't surprise me,' said Dr McMath polishing his spectacles carefully. 'Shouldn't surprise you neither, Hannah. You know what some of those homes were like.'

'Doesn't surprise me at all,' she answered tartly, 'but what I cannot cope with is this here boy just refusing to go to school to learn.'

She shook Jack slightly and then released him. Lucy had gone to stand beside him.

'You won't go to school?' Mrs McMath asked Jack.

He shook his head, his face red with embarrassment. Lucy put her hand in his.

'You have to go to school,' said Miss Chiltern firmly, 'or you can't work with me.'

Jack hung his head.

KEZZIE

:

'Kezzie,' said Lucy. 'Please, Kezzie. Don't make him go. Everyone will call him a "Home Child" or "White Trash". Kezzie, you could teach him. Couldn't you? Please?'

30. A letter from home

Jack was a quick learner and with Lucy's help soon made good progress. Kezzie came through from the kitchen one night leaving them both bent over their books at the table.

Dr McMath folded his newspaper and smiled.

'School over?' he asked.

'Yes,' said Kezzie, sitting down with a sigh. 'He is an intelligent boy. For his education to be neglected for so long is a scandal. These so-called philanthropists, who sent children out here, should be put in jail.'

Mrs McMath put her knitting down.

'Kezzie,' she said gently. 'It was not a bad thing in all cases. For some orphans who were destitute or in a workhouse, it was a unique opportunity.'

'Well,' said Kezzie, 'I can hardly believe it. I would like to meet such a child.'

'You have,' said Sarah McMath, 'two in fact. Andrew and I were Home Children.'

Kezzie sat up in her chair.

Dr McMath looked at his wife with a fond smile. 'We were sent over by Quarrier's Homes in Scotland at the turn of the century.'

Kezzie was astounded. 'You!' She looked from one to the other. 'What happened to you?'

'We were orphans,' said Mrs McMath, 'and I suppose that the home thought that they would give us a fresh start in a new country away from the slums in Glasgow.'

'Do you remember the journey, Sarah?' asked Dr McMath. 'It took eighteen days to get to Halifax, and then the train, a gigantic monster pouring out steam.'

'I remember rats running around in the steerage,' said his wife, 'and seeing whales in the ocean spouting water. It was the most exciting thing that had ever happened to me.'

'I was put on a farm back east,' said the doctor. 'It is much colder there in the winter. The first snowfall was measured in feet not inches. My mattress was a straw tick made from flour bags with a sheet and a blanket. I rose at dawn and worked all day, milking cows, hoeing corn, lifting potatoes, splitting wood, harnessing the horses for ploughing. It was hard work, but the folk were kindly enough.'

'I was sent into domestic service,' said Mrs McMath, 'but the old lady treated me as her own. I was very fortunate. She left me her home when she died, and even though it was mortgaged I started up a boarding house and made more than enough to live on.'

'And then one day,' continued her husband, 'a handsome young fellow came to lodge with you because he was going to college in the town.'

'And he took me out for a buggy ride and went into a field and picked me a bunch of brown-eyed Susans . . .'

They smiled at each other.

' "He is the God that giveth the desolate a home to dwell in," ' murmured Dr McMath.

Kezzie took down the chess set from the shelf by the fire.

The world is a strange place, she thought as she set out the pieces, full of contradictions and conflicting ideas.

A few weeks later a letter arrived for her from her grandfather.

My dear Kezzie
I have received your letters and I am glad that all is well with Lucy and yourself, although I sense that you may have been through difficulties but have not gone into detail. Thank the doctor and his wife on my behalf and tell them I will pass their kindness on to someone else as this is the only way I can repay them. Kezzie, I must tell you that I have had a great promotion and that I have a tenement flat to rent in Clydebank. It is very well appointed with extra space and a toilet inside, which I myself do not consider to be hygienic, but

it is a welcome facility in the winter-time. There is room for yourself and Lucy, a school close by and also a college. There is an Italian café not far away and I have spoken to the owner and he can let you work there at night and you could take courses in the college in daytime. Now, Kezzie, these are my thoughts. However, you sound as though you are very happy in Canada, and Lucy is thriving, and if you decide to make a new life there I will understand. It is a new land and there must be many opportunities, and you will have many friends. So, I will understand if you decide to stay, but if you decide to come back I am here for you. Your ever-loving grandfather.

Kezzie kept the letter in her pocket all day as she worked in the surgery. Her mind was in turmoil. The time had passed so quickly since they had arrived in Waterfoot, and Lucy was now so well that Mrs McMath had been talking of enrolling her in school. Kezzie knew Lucy had taken a very special place in the older woman's heart.

After dinner when they were drinking coffee in the sitting-room Kezzie handed them the letter. The doctor read it slowly and then gave it to his wife. She read it twice and then took her hanky out and blew her nose.

'Kezzie,' said Dr McMath, 'you must decide what you think best. All I would say is, that I too had thought of you studying here and perhaps winning a place at university.' He sighed. 'What will you do?'

'I don't know,' wailed Kezzie. 'I feel I am being torn in two. I cannot take this responsibility.'

'No one else can,' said Sarah McMath.

Kezzie folded her hands in her lap. It was true, she thought. There was no one else to make this decision. Not Dr and Mrs McMath, or her Aunt Bella or Grandfather, a thousand and more miles away. Lucy was too young and vulnerable. She, Kezzie, had to make the decision of a lifetime for both of them.

In the kitchen warming some milk for Lucy before bed, Mrs McMath spoke to Kezzie. 'No matter what you decide there is always a home for both of you here,' she said.

Impulsively Kezzie hugged her.

Kezzie lay in bed that night unable to sleep. Forsythia would be coming out just now in Scotland, bright yellow on brown bush. There would be a great golden carpet of daffodils beneath the trees, and the tops of the hills still covered with snow. The missing of the place and the people was suddenly a physical pain. She placed her hands on her stomach and then across her heart. Until now she had been so occupied with merely keeping Lucy alive she had no time to dwell on her own feelings. Now they came back in a rush, the sound of friends' voices, the calling of children in the dusty village street.

The sight of Bella, always cheerful in spite of troubles, with her little ones clutching at her skirt. And Grandad, she had an image of him in her head, his tall figure with his muffler and cap, and the smell of pipe tobacco. It must have taken courage for him to have written such a letter, releasing her as best he could from any obligation to return.

Except ... there were bonds that you could not break, for instance the one that linked her and Michael Donohoe. The one that had made Matt McPhee turn back on the road to Skye. Kin calling to kin. With a terrible realisation Kezzie knew that if she remained here in Canada then she might never see these people again.

What should she do? Always before, when she had faced trouble, the road had been a hard one to travel but in one way a path was already chosen for her. Now she had to decide. This beautiful country with its great open heart was waiting to welcome them both. And they would prosper here. She knew that as a certainty, as surely as the day followed night. She fell asleep at last, her mind troubled.

She was awoken the next morning by the sound of honking. She went to her little window and pulled aside the curtain. Across the fields on the marshland she could see a flock of geese, unmistakably Canadian geese with the black neck and head, and a broad white band across throat and cheeks.

She watched them for a moment or two as they shifted restlessly about, cackling and bickering with each other.

She opened the window to watch them. It was a

deep instinctive urge that commanded them. Centuries of inbuilt pattern dictated their direction, as each year, winter over, they returned to their breeding grounds. They are going home, she thought suddenly, as I should. She wrapped her arms around herself and leaned out on the windowsill. She *would* go back to Scotland, she decided. When Lucy was well enough to travel they would cross the Atlantic and be reunited with Grandad. At the moment, although she had found Lucy, it was as though her journey had not yet finished. She would go home. It would be a completion.

But she would come back. That she knew also. More than a spoken commitment or a resolute thought, it was an urge within her that she would answer. She had an instinctive feeling that she would return to Canada.

From the marshes there came a great disturbance and flapping of wings as the geese, answering an unseen signal scrambled to be airborne. Kezzie looked above her and watched them finding their direction. The birds formed their long distinctive V shape and turned north. They honked loudly, and it seemed to her, happily, as they headed towards home.